For Alice Horner,
who knows a thing or two about
taking someone under her wing

HATCHED

Gentle Reader—

I am pleased, but nervous, to present this account of my adventures in the human world and what happened to me there.

To give you the story completely, I have woven into my diary (which was originally intended to be quite personal!) many documents and papers that I hope will help you fully understand the terror and the drama of it all.

Gaaah! That sounds a little over the top, doesn't it? Well, my teacher, Master Abelard (whom you will meet later in these pages), has occasionally called me a drama queen.

I will not demean myself by explaining what that means, but I sometimes fear it is true.

On the other wing, I did indeed experience a great deal of terror on this journey. So that is also true.

In addition to my diary, you will find many pages from the journal of a human boy named Bradley Ashango, as well as photographs he took with a strange device called a cell phone. He swears the thing is not magical, merely scientific. I am not entirely convinced of this. It certainly seems magical to me.

Many times Brad and I had written about the same experience, so I trimmed some of our entries to avoid unnecessary repetition. However, nothing has been added! We want you to experience this as we did.

Well, not *entirely* as we did. I suffered a great deal of fear, doubt, and emotional agony during these events. Though I hope you will read with a sympathetic heart, I also hope that the emotional effects will not be as overwhelming for you as they were for me.

One last note: Please excuse my poetry. Master Abelard tells me it is not very good. But it is part of who I am, so I felt it was important to leave it in place.

Yours very sincerely,
Gerald Overflight, Griffin

The Code of the Griffins

I. A griffin is brave and fierce in all situations. The heart quails not, and the beak and talons are ever ready to strike in the name of truth and freedom.

II. Now that Great Alexander has left the human world, and the divine Dante has gone to the Fields of the Blessed, griffins are no more to be seen by humans.

III. We are guardians of treasure, and any item of value placed in a griffin's care, whether it be glittering diamond or hope of heaven, will be protected unto the death. A griffin who fails in this regard is no griffin at all.

IV. The Enchanted Realm is our home and haven, and we go no more to the human world.

V. We live in a state of joy and gratitude that we have been given the gift of the sky. And we are ever thankful for these treasures: the power of wings, the ferocity of heart, the strength of limb, and the purity of intent that make us, now and evermore . . . GRIFFINS!

This is the Code of the Griffins, as given to us by Izzikiah Wildbeak and written down by Josiah Cloudclaws in *The Griffinagria*.

Reader—

I put in the Code so you would understand the kind of pressure I was facing. We grifflings ("grifflings" is the word for young griffins) are given a copy of this document on our seventh Hatchday and ordered to memorize it. Our elders expect that within two weeks we will be able to recite word for word any item on the list when asked.

"Gerald, give me number three," some grown-up will demand, and I have to be ready to spew it back.

Anyway, now that you've seen the Code, it's time to show you my actual diary, which starts on the next page. You will always be able to tell when it's me writing, because I begin my entries with the full day and date. (Brad claims this is overly fussy, but I think it's the proper way to do it.)

For ease of reading, I have converted the dates of events in the Enchanted Realm to match corresponding days in the human world.

You're welcome.

—G.O.

Friday, June 19

This was a bad day, mostly due to the continued teasing from my rotten siblings, who claim I am not a true griffin.

This wounds me.

In fact, today it made me so mad that I wrote a poem about Cyril:

Higgledy-piggledy,
Berries and tarts,
Cyril's the king
Of huge stinky farts!

That made me feel better.

I'm going to try to write a poem every day. They seem to help me get my feelings out.

To check the claims of the SS (Stupid Siblings) that I am not a true griffin, I looked up "griffins" in our family's copy of the Encyclopedia Enchantica.

Having read what the EE has to say, my response is "What a lot of unicorn poop!"

Encyclopedia Enchantica

GRIFFINS

The griffin is a creature of enormous power, blessed with the head and wings of an eagle and the hindquarters of a lion. The upper sections of the front legs are also lionlike. However, they taper down to become more birdlike, finally ending in the fierce talons of an eagle.

The only exception to the eagle/lion mix is the griffin's ears, which are long and horselike, though they thrust out sideways rather than standing straight up as a horse's do. This can add an oddly comic touch to a griffin's otherwise dignified and ferocious appearance.

As the eagle is the lord of all birds and the lion the king of beasts, the griffin, which combines the two forms, is considered the monarch of all creatures.

Griffins (also known as "griffons" or "gryphons," but here we use the preferred spelling) are often guardians of treasure. They have a deep and abiding love for gold, jewels, and all manner of precious things.

They also guard reputation, a different kind of treasure, one that is uniquely valuable.

A griffin's claw is said to have medicinal properties, and a feather from its wings is supposedly able to restore sight to the blind. (It is not clear whether the latter is actually true.)

Because of its mix of parts, the griffin is seen as having a dual nature. For some it is a symbol of the divine. For others it is ferocity on the wing, the very sight of which terrifies all but the bravest of men.

Indeed, the griffin community divided over these very matters in the Great Griffin Schism of 1792, which led to the establishment of the American Aerie.

Heloise Batwing, Dwarf
Lead Scholar, Guild Hall

Friday, June 19 (continued)

All right, I'll admit the encyclopedia describes what I *look like* well enough, right down to my silly ears.

But that whole thing about being ferocious?

HAH! And again, HAH!

Okay, I suppose a lot of griffins really are ferocious.

Okay, maybe *most* griffins are ferocious.

Unfortunately, I don't qualify. Except, of course, when I get really angry. But that never lasts for long and usually ends in tears.

Mine.

Good grief! Does what I just wrote mean that my rotten siblings are right when they say I'm not a true griffin? Great Izzikiah, maybe it's so. Right now I do not feel ferocious.

Mostly what I feel is frettingly nervous.

I'd write a poem about it, but I've already done one for today.

The reason I am nervous is simple: In only twenty-four days, my Tenth Hatchday (which is supposed to be a major holiday) will arrive. Alas, for reasons I would rather not discuss, this is not my real Hatchday, simply the one we *count* as my Hatchday.

The problem is, I must acquire a True Treasure by then

or be declared not a True Griffin . . . this time not by my stinky sibs but by Artoremus Lashtail, the High Lord of the Griffin Stronghold of the Northern Quarter. And it will happen in front of everyone we know, at the Hatchday Gathering at the Great Cavern.

I cannot bear to think of Dad's disappointment if I do not succeed in this. But I have no idea what to get or where to get it. I have been fretting about this, but I have not been *thinking* about it as I should. This is because treasure does not interest me as much as it is supposed to.

I really am a very bad griffin.

The situation is so awful that I am seriously considering running away!

But where? Pretty much anywhere I go in the Enchanted Realm they would find me. That leaves only the human world.

But that idea is too horrible to even consider!

June 20

Dear Mom,

I'm writing to ask if Brad can stay with you again this summer. He had a great time last year, and right now Manhattan looks to be even hotter than it was then. (Global warming . . . a topic on which we actually agree!)

To be honest, it's not just the heat. It's been a bad year for Brad. He's had to deal with a fair amount of bullying at school. Not as bad as at the old school, but even so . . .

Also, he's really been missing his dad. It's been over three years, but sometimes I think it's even worse for him now than it was when it happened. Maybe it's just that the older a boy gets, the more he needs to have his dad around. Or at least some man in his life. So I'm thinking maybe your buddy Herb will be good for him.

Look, Mom, I know the two of us still aren't getting along that well. But Brad loves his "Bibi," and I think this would be really good for him.

What do you say?

Love,
Delia

Sunday, June 21

Sometimes I wish I were an only child!
Seriously.
It's not that I don't love my sibs.
Well, in a way.
If I really, really try . . .

Boogers and frog guts,
A shred and a shard,
Loving my siblings
Is pretty darn hard!

This love thing is a mystery, and the kind of question my teacher, Master Abelard, likes to discuss. Should you have to *try* to love someone? Shouldn't it come naturally?

He can talk about that kind of thing for hours.

Love or not, natural or not, I can't take Cyril's bossiness and Violet's snippiness any longer.

It didn't help that Violet had her pegasus friend Aerilinn over today. The two of them are so snotty when they're together! (And it is well known that there is nothing snottier than a snotty pegasus!) I wish I had never accepted the feather from Aerilinn's right wing that Violet gave me on our eighth Hatchday. It truly is a thing of beauty and a fine treasure. But it wasn't worth what I've had to put up with from the two of them ever since.

What I wish even more is that Mom hadn't slipped last month and told my brat brother and snip of a sister the true story of our Hatchday.

Days.

I know Mom regrets this now that she sees how they use it against me (though she only sees a small part of it). But there's no taking it back, and ever since it came out, my sibs have been so full of themselves it makes me want to yark up a hair ball.

Which just shows how annoying Violet and Cyril are, since I *hate* puking up hair balls. It is impossible to have any sense of dignity while you are doing it! Okay, I know. Cats of all sizes cough up hair balls all the time. But even though I have the body of a lion, having the head of an eagle makes spitting up those wretched, soggy globs of fur truly disgusting. I especially hate it when they get caught on my beak and dangle there like giant juicy boogers!

Stupid hair balls.

Oh well. At least I have talons in front and claws in back. That is kind of cool, since it makes me extremely dangerous.

Yes! That is me! Gerald the Invincible!

Blarg.

I am about as invincible as a daisy.

Anyway, between Violet and Aerilinn teasing me this

morning, and that wing whap Cyril landed on the back of my head this afternoon, today was the last straw. I have decided for sure. I am going to run away to the human world.

Yes, the human world!

I can just imagine Violet gasping in horror and telling me this will be a violation of the Code of the Griffins. Which is actually true. But how griffinlike is it for them to pick on me the way they do? Don't they have any sense of family honor?

I can also imagine Cyril (or, more technically, Cyril-the-Pain) correcting me to point out that a griffin would not "run away," he would "*fly* away." He is so literal-minded that it is useless to make puns at him. For example, if I tried to point out that Fly Away would be a good name for an insect repellent, he would never get it.

I like making puns. Alas, Master Abelard claims it is a bad habit and not something I should indulge in.

Well, pun or not, bad habit or not, I *am* going to fly away!

Once I am free of my brat brother and snippy sister, and no longer under my parents' wings (so to speak), I can start developing my own true life.

If only the idea weren't so scary!

But if I don't do this, I'll be a griffin wuss forever!

June 22

Mrs. Delia Ashango
<street address redacted for reasons of privacy—ed.>
New York, NY 10023
Re: Summer Assignment for Bradley

Dear Mrs. Ashango,

This is to confirm our conversation regarding summer work for Bradley. First, let me repeat what I told you in our conference: Bradley's teachers are unanimously in favor of letting him continue at the school, but *only* under the conditions we have discussed.

Regarding those conditions: As you know, WIPS prides itself on holding its students to the highest standards. According to test scores from his previous school, Bradley is one of the more gifted students we have had the pleasure to accept in recent years. Alas, he is also one of the most unmotivated. Though he glides through his work, he rarely exerts himself. In this regard, he is a bad influence on his fellow students. We need to see a serious commitment to "Pursuit of Excellence" if Bradley is to return to campus for his sixth-grade year.

For this reason we have mandated, and you and Bradley

have consented, that he will keep a journal this summer. He is to make entries in this journal no less than four days a week, and they must consist of at least three paragraphs of at least three sentences each.

To avoid having Bradley put this off and then write several entries during the last few days of summer, the journal entries are to be sent to Mr. Delong every Saturday.

Failure to adhere to this agreement will result in Bradley being unable to return next year.

We truly do not wish to lose Bradley as a student. However, WIPS has a long waiting list with many applicants. Please do not doubt that dozens of bright young students are eager to take your son's place in our hallowed halls.

I hope you will not mistake my tone in this letter. I have endeavored to be firm but polite. If I have failed in that, I apologize.

Hopefully, and in the spirit of positivity,

Vincent Castle

Headmaster, WIPS

Tuesday, June 23

I need to talk about my teacher, Master Abelard. Gracious, I could not even keep this diary if not for him! He is the one who taught me how to pluck one of my own feathers (ouch!), dip it into ink, and use it to write upon the page.

The first thing I have to say is that he is brilliant.

The second thing I have to say is that, unfortunately, he is a gnome.

It is not that *I* have anything against gnomes! But because of Master Abelard's gnomehood I have had to endure endless teasing from Cyril and his friends about "Gerald and his tiny teacher."

When, oh when, will people stop judging beings on the basis of size?

The sibs, of course, didn't care to have a tutor. They would rather remain ignorant. Which is my inspiration for today's poem:

Hobbilty-pobbilty
Bubbles and soup,
How did I ever
End up in this group?

Alas, Master Abelard says this kind of thing is not true poetry. He calls it "doggerel," which I guess is not a good thing.

I must try to do better.

Despite his criticism of my poems, Master Abelard is the wisest, kindest, and most educated being I have ever met. The problem is that because he is so small, people tend to look down on him. Well, you have to look down to *see* him, of course, because he is only six inches tall. (Not counting his red hat, which adds another two inches to his height.) What I mean is that people (including my rotten siblings) treat him with scorn *because* of his size.

If only they could understand how wise he is!

For a complete picture, I will add that he dresses in traditional gnome clothing, with a blue coat buckled about the waist, brown trousers, and high leather boots. A short knife is strapped to his belt. He has, of course, a thick white beard that flows about a third of the way down his chest. His eyes are bright blue, and his nose is rounded, as are his cheeks. Beware those blue eyes! When he is angered (and, I will admit, he does have a bit of a temper), they flash in ways that make me want to hide my head under my wing . . . despite the fact that I am large enough to swallow him in a single gulp!

He can also be extremely sarcastic when I do or say something foolish.

Which happens with distressing frequency.

But usually he is kind and gentle.

Oh! I should mention that he is a remarkable artist. Well, *I* think he is remarkable. He claims that being able to draw is one of the basic disciplines and should be part of the education of all humanoid creatures. (By which he means gnomes, dwarfs, elves, brownies, goblins, and so on . . . basically anyone with hands. Which I do not have.)

Despite my lack of fingers, Master Abelard has tried to teach me to draw. Alas, I have no gift in that direction. My drawings stink.

I should add that despite his temper and his gift of sarcasm, my teacher has been remarkably patient in the matter of my lack of skill on this front.

Master A, as I sometimes call him, has been working with me for three years now, and my heart is fierce with love for him.

To be honest (as one should be in one's diary), I don't think he would disapprove if I ran away, despite the shame it would bring on my family. Sometimes I even think he is hinting that I should do it! I know he is disgusted by the way Cyril and Violet treat me.

Blarg. I hate emotions. They make everything so complicated!

I can't take this anymore. Tomorrow I am leaving, and that's final.

Why my teacher does not think highly of my drawings.

Abelard Chronicus
Suite 217, Gnome Hall,
University Enchantica, North American Division

June 23

Henrik Flutternight
Dean of Gnomic Studies
University Enchantica
North American Division

Dear Henrik,

I wanted to let you (and only you!) know that if all goes well I will soon be leaving the Enchanted Realm. I have been watching Gerald closely, and I believe my nudging has worked. I am fairly certain the griffling is finally planning to run away to the human world!

I will go with him, of course, since that was the point of all the hints and prods I've been administering. What I am not sure of yet is whether I will tell him I am planning to come along or simply stow away in that travel sack I made for him last month.

As you well know, I have solid reasons for going, both academic and personal. And now that things have turned so against me here at the university (by all that is enchanted, I hate academic politics!), this seems a fitting moment for some self-imposed exile.

If nothing else, it may be wise for me to, so to speak, "get out of town" for a while. But it's more than that. With luck, this adventure, perilous though it might be, will provide the payoff for nearly two centuries of research . . . research I have shared with only you ever since it was proclaimed forbidden.

Did I mention that I hate academic politics? What small minds it takes to declare a topic forbidden! How can we take ourselves seriously as a university if we put things beyond the realm of study?

Sorry. I know you are already well aware of my feelings on the matter.

Anyway, I am sending this so that if I do disappear you will not be left wondering what happened to me. As you are my one true friend here, I would not want to do that to you.

My sole regret in all this is that I truly do wish I were as good and wise as Gerald believes me to be.

I feel quite guilty about the way I am about to use the griffling.

Sincerely,

Abelard

Enchanted Realm

The Study of Magic Is the Study of Life

Memo to All Department Heads:
Forbidden Topics at the University Enchantica

Following is the current list of topics considered off-limits for discussions, seminars, research papers, and general scholarship, as per order of PRISS (Prohibited Research and Instruction Security Services).

Topics are arranged in order of sensitivity, from lowest to highest.

Also included is a notation of the reason for each topic's banning.

1) The origin of unicorns
   (Mythic sensitivity)
2) The meaning of EXTOOMBIA!
   (Obvious reasons, too delicate to cite. Please, don't even think about it!)
3) How the Transcendental Curtain is maintained
   (Security concerns)
4) Why fairies have wings
   (Cultural sensitivity, secret history)

5) Whether monkeys can actually fly out of someone's nether region*
   (Distasteful)
6) Who put the bop in the bop shoo bop shoo bop?
   (Indicates disturbing obsession with the human world)
7) The creation of centaurs
   (Pointless speculation, trigger issues)
8) Wood elves versus high elves
   (Political issues, cultural sensitivity, potential eruption of warfare)
9) Dragon digestive systems
   (Obvious safety concerns)
10) The Lost City of Batavia
   (Security concerns, cultural sensitivity, political pressure, heresy)

Please remind your staff that these topics are *not* to be discussed or taught! To do so is to risk termination of position, dismissal from the university, and possible banishment.

Egbert Waffle, Gremlin
Dean of Discipline and Enforcement

* *"Nether region" means "butt." I had to ask Master A, so I figured I should explain it here. You're welcome.*— G.O.

Wednesday, June 24

Despite my vow to leave today, I am still here. For the entire day I did nothing but dither about going, which is embarrassing, since dithering is ungriffinlike.

I suppose running away to the human world will also be ungriffinlike. On the other hand, it would be incredibly bold, which is *very* griffinlike.

Part of me is starting to love the idea of fleeing to the human world. In fact, in my heart I wonder if the boldness of defying the Code and entering that forbidden place might be the thing that could finally undo the stain of my Hatchday and earn my father's respect.

Festering pestering
Dithers and doubt,
I hate that my father
Wonders what I'm about!

Wow. That one was kind of painful to write.

Ah well, Master A has often told me an artist has to suffer. He says teachers often suffer, too, and that this is true for him when he reads my poetry.

That feels harsh, but I appreciate the high standards he sets for me.

As regards suffering, I suppose I would suffer greatly if I ran away. So perhaps it would be good for my writing to do this.

On the other wing, when I think of the rules I would break and the dangers I would encounter, the idea terrifies me. (Very UNgriffinlike.)

On the other other wing (was there ever a three-winged griffin?), what if I could find a really amazing treasure in the human world? I must find one in less than three weeks or suffer Unendurable Shame.

I am starting to panic about the matter. I do not like shame, and Unendurable Shame would be . . . well, unendurable!

The thing is, until now my treasures have all been given to me. I have no idea how to go about obtaining one on my own!

I cannot fault Master A for not teaching me this. It is entirely a griffin thing and should have come from my family.

Truly our educational system leaves much to be desired.

Well, it's silly to worry about the treasure thing. If I run away, it's not with the thought that I'll be coming back! The whole point of running away is to be gone!

REGARDING THE ACQUISITION AND MAINTENANCE OF A GRIFFIN HOARD

From *A Field Guide to Griffins*
By Percival Rendslash, Keeper of the Griffin Registry

It is an essential aspect of griffins that they are guardians of treasure. For this reason it is expected that every griffin will, as he or she matures, gather and maintain a personal hoard. It has long been proven that fidelity to this task is crucial to the growth and development of a griffling's character.

However, the griffling does not have to do this on his or her own. By tradition, on the first nine anniversaries of a griffin's hatching, specific relatives are expected to bring the youngster an item to add to his or her hoard. Families usually have an established order to these gifts. In almost all cases the first-year treasure comes from the griffling's parents, the second hoard-gift from the mother of the mother, and the third from the father of the father.

After that the order of gifting varies from aerie to aerie but is strictly adhered to within the aerie.

This all changes on the Tenth Hatchday, when it is expected that a young griffin will have acquired a new treasure by him- or herself and will display it to the community at the Hatchday celebration. Upon doing so, he or she becomes a "griffer"—the stage between child and full-fledged adult.

Failure to obtain this "growing up" treasure is seen as a sign that the griffling is not fit to join the Greater Aerie. **The shame is great and creates a permanent blot on the family reputation.**

Thursday, June 25

    Still here.
    Too depressed for poetry.

From the Journal of Bradley Ashango

(Summer Assignment)

6/26 (Fri.)

This is my summer journal. This is the first entry. I will try to do a good job.

Tomorrow I go to my grandmother's house. She lives in the country. I bet she will have cookies.

I hope my mother will be all right without me. She might eat too much. I hope she does not get fat.

(3 paragraphs, 3 sentences each.)

6/26

Holy flying pizza sticks! It seriously makes me laugh to think I have to keep that silly journal for school.

"Three paragraphs of three sentences each."

I've been sentenced to sentences!

This isn't an assignment; it's an insult to my intelligence. I've carried a pocket journal for two years now, ever since Dad . . . well, ever since. Some days I write pages, not paragraphs!

So I will send Mr. Delong my short journal and keep the long version for myself. And that's de long and de short of it!

HEH. Sometimes I amuse myself so much I could burst!

Anyway, here are the thoughts I'm thinking right now: First off, I love my new smartphone, even though I suspect that it was a guilt gift because Mom is feeling bad about shipping me off to the Catskills for the summer.

I just took my first selfie.

Secondly, the guilt gift was hardly necessary

(though I happily accepted it), since I am totally jazzed that I'll be going back to Bibi Riddlehoover's for the summer!

Here's my own guilty thing: It will be a huge relief to be away from Mom for a while. It's not that I don't love her. I do. Of course I do. But emotionally speaking, she's a total mess.

On the other hand, both of us have good reason for being messed up.

Well, never mind. That's one thing I *don't* want to write about now.

Or ever, if I can manage it.

What I do want to note down is my hope that something cool, something magical, will happen this summer.

For the first time in a long time I honestly think that's possible. Underneath all the touristy stuff about the "enchanted" Catskill Mountains, there really is something mystical about the place. When you get away from the towns, out into farm territory where Bibi lives, you can *sense* it in the land . . . sense it in every nook and hollow.

And when you go into the forest, it feels like *anything* is possible. Rambling through the woods that surround Bibi's farm is one of my favorite things ever. The place feels old and strange and alive in a way I can't begin to describe.

I don't think this sense of magic is just my imagination. After all, this is where "Rip Van Winkle" and "The Legend of Sleepy Hollow" are set.

My school is named for Washington Irving, the guy

who wrote those two stories, which are so famous that even though most people have never actually read them they know the basic plots. I *did* read both of them this spring, and I have to say that they are even weirder than people realize.

They're also funny, in a grown-up kind of way.

Mostly they make it clear that the Catskills are a place where weirdness happens.

I should also add that Mr. Irving was way more cool than my school has ever dreamed of being . . . a total snark-meister.

(I bet he could write a hilarious story about how WIPS is run.)

Anyway, given what I experienced while I was at Bibi's last summer, I would say my hope for something cool happening is not totally crazy.

Unless I was hallucinating that night, which is possible.

Though I am excited to be going back, I have to admit (in these pages only) that I am also a little frightened.

That one night was just so weird!

★   ★

From the Notebook of Abelard Chronicus

◇◇◇◇◇◇◇◇◇◇◇◇◇◇◇◇◇◇◇◇

June 26

Today, as scheduled, I used Falcon Flight Services to carry me to the Overflight family's aerie so I could work with Gerald.

I do not like to think of myself as timid, but even after all these years I am not entirely comfortable riding those birds. I remain acutely aware that I am of a size they would consider appropriate for dinner.

To calm my fears, I remind myself that if the falcon couriers were to start eating passengers on a regular basis, the service would soon be out of business. Discipline is strictly imposed—which is why it has been over fifty years since there was what is referred to as "an incident."

So I suppose I shouldn't worry.

Even so . . .

Well, that is beside the point. More important to note is that my campaign of hints to get Gerald to consider scarpering off to the human world seems to have faltered. I thought I had pushed him into it, but I can tell he is wavering.

And dithering, of course.

I am fond of the boy, but he does dither.

May the Powers Bright forgive me for using the griffling this way. But my heart's deepest desire, which is not for wealth or fame or honors but for one true reconnection, depends on making this journey happen.

That is, assuming that everything I have worked out in nearly two hundred years of study and research is correct.

Drew this to soothe my nerves while waiting for Gerald.

Friday, June 26

Still here. But now I have a reason for delaying, and it's not just that leaving the Enchanted Realm will be a total violation of the Code.

The reason is that I have come to the conclusion that I need to do more planning.

This is partly because of the visit from Master A today. It was a tricky situation. I did not want to tell him I was intending to leave the Enchanted Realm, because he would be honor-bound to stop me. But I did talk about how Mom and Dad had always warned us about leaving.

In response, Master A said that this was typical parental exaggeration and exiting the Realm is not nearly as easy as some people seem to think.

Which alerted me that I need to do some research on how to get out of here! Our parents have spent so much time cautioning the three of us against straying out of the Realm that I got the impression it would be so easy you might do it by accident. But now that I am thinking about leaving, I realize I have no idea how to go about it!

Another reason for my delay is that I am not certain I can bear to leave Master A.

Could I really survive in the human world without my teacher?

Here is today's poem:

Framadoo-blamadoo,
My teacher's the best.
I hope he don't think
That I'm just a pest.

Drat. The grammar is bad in that one.
Is grammar important in poetry?
Probably.
So that's annoying. I would prefer to get along without grammar if I could manage it.

I could also get along without my stupid brother. I swear, if Cyril calls me "Geraldine" one more time I am going to pluck his pinfeathers! The fact that I have been studying sky ballet, which is graceful and extremely athletic, does not mean I am a girl! But Cyril Stupidhead thinks anyone who would rather skydance than play Seven-Griffin Air Battle is a sissy.

Gaaah!

But what if I really am a sissy? The truth is that what I am thinking of doing frightens me from the sharp point of my beak to the tufted tip of my tail.

That is not good. It is not becoming for a griffin to feel fear!

On the other wing, Master Abelard once told me that "he who feels no fear can never be courageous." He says that only the stupid are never afraid. *Overcoming* your fear is the true mark of courage.

So take that, Cyril, you never-scaredy-pants. How can you be brave if you've never been afraid?

As for me, I've got the fear part down pat.

Now all I have to do is overcome it.

THE LOST CITY OF BATAVIA

From GNOMISH!
A Collection of Essays on
the Unofficial History of the Gnomes

One of the great unsolved mysteries of the gnome world is the Lost City of Batavia.

In brief, at some point in the early 1700s (as humans mark the years) a small but thriving community of gnomes, one well connected to other villages and cities through the vast network of tunnels that had been built over the centuries, disappeared.

Though it may sound dramatic, the word "disappeared" is the most correct term. If the stories are to be believed, one day Batavia was there, the next day it was not. Oh, the homes themselves remained, along with a great deal of what was in them. But the gnomes themselves had just . . . vanished, with no word of why or how or where. No signs of bloodshed or violence were found. The very lack of those things made the situation all the more mystifying.

Of course, that is *if* the stories are to be believed.

Many theories for the city's disappearance have been put forward over the years. Some think the population was enslaved by a wicked sorcerer. Others believe they were fleeing some great scandal. A small number of people have claimed that the Batavians discovered an item of enormous significance and power and chose to go into hiding to protect it.

There have been hints and rumors that the vanished gnomes departed to the New World on one of the ships taking settlers to the Hudson River Valley. However, no reliable proof of this has ever been offered, and given the edicts from the emperor at around that time, the very idea seems laughable.

To this day, the fate of the Batavian gnomes remains a mystery that perplexes historians. At least three gnomish novels have explored the story. They have been popular but are considered trashy at best by more distinguished critics.

The fact that the gnome king has a standing offer of five thousand golden perkles for anyone who solves the puzzle has helped keep the question fresh in gnomish minds.

Abelard Chronicus
Professor of Gnomics
University Enchantica
North American Division

Enchanted Realm

The Study of Magic Is the Study of Life

⎯⎯◈◇◈⎯⎯

From: Office of Discipline & Enforcement,
      University Enchantica, North American Division
Date: June 26
To: Abelard Chronicus, Gnome, Gnome Hall,
      University Enchantica, North American Division

Dear Professor Chronicus,

    That you allowed your essay regarding a certain historical mystery (which I shall not name here!) to be published in *GNOMISH! A Collection of Essays on the Unofficial History of the Gnomes* has recently come to our attention.

    We were startled—nay, shocked!—to see that you had written this, much less allowed it to see the light of day. To say that we were displeased is an understatement.

    This is a final warning. Any additional pursuit of this subject, which is clearly on the Forbidden Topics List, will result in severe disciplinary action, most likely expulsion from the university and the termination of your teaching career.

           Sincerely,
           Egbert Waffle, Gremlin
           Dean of Discipline and Enforcement

Saturday, June 27

I have made my packing list.

This is good, as it helps me feel that my plan to depart is more real.

The list is actually quite brief. Here it is:

Diary (without it I would go mad!)
Inkpot (so I can write in the diary)
Treasures (duh!)
Encyclopedia Enchantica (condensed edition)

The treasures, of course, I *must* take, as it is my job to guard them. I have nine, one given to me each year on the anniversary of my hatching. Well, on the day I was *supposed* to hatch.

I am still horrified that Mom told Cyril and Violet what actually happened that day.

Those days.

Once the sibs heard the story, it was nothing but ammunition for them to tease me with. Mom has spoken to them about it many times. Sometimes quite harshly. But once she is out of earshot they ignore what she has said and continue to harass me.

Snickety-snackety,
My siblings are pains.
So what if they tease me?
It shows they lack brains!

Hmmm. That one is not very nice. I wonder if it is acceptable to write mean poetry. Maybe yes, if it's about someone who is being mean to you?

I shall have to discuss this with Master Abelard.

Moving on to more important things, I still have to deal with the matter of this year's treasure! I have been fussing for at least six months now over what I might acquire. I want it to be special and awesome and amazing, to show my siblings and my dad that I am more than they think, better than they realize.

Which is all very good . . . except I have no idea how I am going to do that!

And I only have two weeks and four days left to try!

Oh dither dither dither. Why in the world am I worrying about the Hatchday celebration when I don't intend to be here for it?! I hate the thought of missing it, but it's likely if I *am* here, I will suffer enormous humiliation.

GAAAAHHHH! Why can't I choose just one thing to worry about?!

I really am a creature of two parts.

The Treasures of Gerald Overflight

(Annotated list, as recorded in the Griffin Registry)

Following is a list of the items currently in the hoard of Gerald Overflight. Also noted is the source of each item, as well as occasional comments on the gifts themselves.

<u>Year 1:</u> One small diamond, wept by the dragon Fiona for her lost love; given by Gerald's parents, Reginald and Cecelia Overflight.

Note: Considering Gerald's sensitive and overwrought nature, this gem-tear from a lovelorn dragon proved to be particularly appropriate. It does, however, raise the question of whether the gift suited the griffling or if it in fact helped determine his personality.

As with most jewels that are part of an individual hoard, the diamond is stored in a small silk bag made by the spider people of the Great Southern Forest.

<u>Year 2:</u> One large ruby from the hilt of an ancient Roman sword; presented by Lucretia Broadwing, maternal grandmother of Gerald.

<u>Year 3:</u> First edition of *The Adventures of Tom Sawyer*;

provided by Mortimer Overflight, paternal grandfather of Gerald.

Year 4: Golden ring reputed to have been worn by the Queen of Sheba; given by the Granite Valley Trolls, family friends of the Overflights.

Note: The Overflight family has a particularly close relationship with the Granite Valley Trolls, which began when the Overflights rescued a troddler who had become stranded on a cliff.

Year 5: Silver dagger from the recently discovered Elkwood Hoard, possibly handcrafted by the dwarf Shirakuze; brought by Gerald's uncle Mordecai Overflight.

Note: Some complained that this was extravagant.

Year 6: Quill pen used by William Shakespeare while writing *Titus Andronicus;* obtained by Gerald's tutor, Abelard Chronicus, gnome.

Note: There is some debate as to whether this was genuine. Taking into account the somewhat unsavory reputation that has developed around Gnome Chronicus, this is not surprising.

Year 7: Brass armband worn by Alexander the Great; given by Gerald's brother, Cyril.

Note: For several years Alexander the Great wore a new armband each day, giving the previous day's armband to the griffins in honor of their mutual agreements. These armbands are ancient treasures but not terribly rare. A common first sibling gift.

<u>Year 8:</u> Feather from the wing of the pegasus Aerilinn; given by Gerald's sister, Violet.

<u>Year 9:</u> Three-thousand-year-old figurine of Ishtar, carved in ivory. From ancient Babylon; given by Artoremus Lashtail, High Lord of the Griffin Stronghold of the Northern Quarter.

Alexander's armband

ALEXANDER AND THE GRIFFINS

From *The Secret History of Alexander the Great*
By Charles Smart, Dwarf, Professor of Hidden History,
University Enchantica

Alexander Griffin-Friend (or, as he is known in the human world, Alexander the Great) is one of the most remarkable figures in the history of Griffindom.

The story most often told by humans about the connection between Alexander and the griffins is that he captured a pair of griffins and forced them to draw a chariot that would carry him to the skies.

As usual, the truth is more complicated. Briefly it is this: In his restless urge to conquer new territory, Alexander marched his army north, where he came to the realm of the griffins, who were wing-deep in their war with the Arimaspians (gigantic, ferocious humanoid creatures, each with but a single eye glaring out at the world from the center of its forehead).

In return for Alexander's help in defeating the Arimaspians, the Grand Aerie of Hyperborea pledged that two griffins would always be at the great man's service. To this pledge the griffins remained ever faithful.

It is true that a brief breach in the relations between

Alexander and the griffins occurred when, in an excess of daring, Alexander urged a team to carry him to the very heavens. That adventure did not end well. However, the rift that followed was resolved when Alexander offered a gracious apology and a generous gift.

Aside from this disruption, the relationship between Alexander and the griffins remained close and cordial to his very last day. Indeed, a griffin guard of honor stood watch at his funeral!

Given his grace of form, blazing courage, ferocity of heart, and desire to soar beyond what is thought possible, Alexander might well have been a griffin in human form.

Sunday, June 28

Great fluttering ear tufts! I may not be able to do this after all.

By "do this," I mean "run away."

I just did some research on how to leave the Enchanted Realm, mostly in a book that I'm not supposed to read. (I would feel guilty about this, but Master A believes with something approaching ferocity that knowledge should not be hidden away.)

While I agree that knowledge should not be hidden, what I found today was fairly horrifying!

WAYS TO PASS FROM THE ENCHANTED REALM TO THE HUMAN REALM

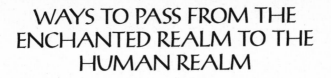

From *Forbidden Knowledge of the Enchanted Realm*
Compiled by Ethelred the Obnoxious, Goblin

Despite the Great Separation, the matter of passing from the Enchanted Realm to the human world (and vice versa) remains a topic of intense interest to beings on both sides of the Transcendental Curtain.

The first thing to state, though it may seem obvious, is that it is generally easier to leave the Enchanted Realm than it is to enter it . . . though in the case of humans there is great variability in the matter. And, of course, once a human *has* penetrated the Realm, he or she may find it quite difficult to depart.

Complicating things is the fact that methods of transit vary from being to being. For those in the human world, the most well-known method of entering the Realm is to go three times widdershins around a church. (That is to say, counterclockwise, keeping the church always to your left.) It is important to note that this generally requires a password. Alas, it is forbidden to write this word, and I would suffer great penalties were I to do so.

Passage also depends on the mood the Realm is in. Sometimes a mortal is allowed to enter unexpectedly.

This is not always a good thing.

Obviously, if the supplicant is *from* the Enchanted Realm, no password is required. Furthermore, any accompanying humans can transit with him, her, or it.

For the creatures of the Shadow Sea, such as mermaids and selkies, there is usually an underwater cave involved. Krakens, however, are no longer allowed to make the passage at all. Given their size and voracious appetites, the possibility of discovery is all too likely.

For the Greater Beasts of the surface world (dragons, unicorns, griffins, etc.), passage has been made more difficult than for smaller beings. This is because their presence in the human world is more easily detected and thus potentially more disruptive. For these creatures, certain key places can act as passage points. A sacred tree, for example, may function much the same way as a church, with a trip about it three times widdershins opening the way. Also, some caves open onto both worlds: Enter from one world, walk through, exit into the other. However, most of those passage points have been sealed over the past century as the two worlds continue to grow more separate.

It is rumored (but not confirmed to the satisfaction of this writer) that reaching a certain velocity of flight—one that stretches the flier to the absolute limit—will sometimes pierce the barrier.

Another method requires an act of courage or faith, as in flying headfirst at full speed toward a stone wall that has been designated as a passage point.

The problem with this method is that it requires not only the right spot but also sufficient belief. The lack of either of these can result in a very painful failure and, usually, death.

Sunday, June 28 (continued)

So unless I can find one of those magical trees or caves that the book talks about, to reach the human world I will have to fly headfirst into a stone wall, believing while I do so that I will magically pass through it!

This reminds me of a story Mom used to tell, called "The Little Griffin Who Could." I should probably chant "I think I can, I think I can, I think I can . . ." while I fly at top speed into a sheer rock wall!

If I "think I can" hard enough, I will make it through to the human world.

If I *don't* believe hard enough, it's SPLAT! and good-bye Gerald.

Probably I should just stay home.

Here is today's poem, which is pretty depressing:

Stay at home, never roam.
Just a stick in the mud,
Gerald, a mighty griffin,
Turned out to be a dud.

NO! I will not let that happen. I must go!

It is not just that I need to be away from my stooopid siblings, who think I am timid and fearful. What they do not understand is that my heart is wild and free and longs to roam far beyond what they can begin to imagine, just as Izzikiah Wildbeak does in *The Griffinagria*. Of course, my sibs wouldn't know about that, for the simple reason that they are not readers. Of the three of us, only I know the full story of the most wonderful griffin of them all.

Silly siblings. They have no idea what they're missing by not reading.

I must make plans.

(Summer Assignment)

6/29 (Mon.)

Yesterday I left the city for my grandmother's house. I went on a Greyhound bus. It was smelly.

The bus left from Port Authority. Three hours later it got to Vande Velde's Landing. My grandmother was waiting for me.

I hope I will have a good summer. I love my grandmother. She has raspberry bushes, but her farm is in bad shape.

(3 paragraphs, 3 sentences each,
including 1 compound sentence.)

6/29

The bus ride to Vande Velde's Landing was about as enjoyable as week-old meatballs with cabbage sauce. That was mostly because the whole process made me feel like a little kid. To begin with, since I am "underage" (according to the bus company), Mom had to fill out an Unaccompanied-Child Form and take it to the customer service window, where we had to wait in a long line. The clerk gave us that look I am so tired of seeing, the one where I can tell he's trying to figure out why someone as white as my mother has a kid as dark as me. It was so annoying I wanted to scream.

When we were finally done with the UCF we had to stand in another line so I could actually get on the bus.

Mom had to stand with me, of course, and she kept fretting about some appointment she had to get to. So I guess she wasn't that worried about sending her firstborn (not to mention her *only* born) off on a bus full of strangers. Okay, I wasn't worried, either. But aren't moms supposed to fuss at times like this?

It made the good-bye kiss I had to endure before she would let me climb on the bus all the more ridiculous.

Before we started out, the driver made a speech about how everyone had better stay quiet and not play loud music or talk too much. She made it clear that if she didn't like the way you were acting, she would throw yer butt off the bus. I had a feeling she could do it, too . . . even to some of the big guys!

I was sitting next to a not-big guy, a skinny dude from India who was heading upstate for a summer job. His name was Aamir and he's been in America for less than a year.

This was the best part of the trip, since Aamir didn't mind when I pestered him with all kinds of questions about Mumbai, which is where he came from. I liked talking to him, especially because Bibi and I are huge fans of Bollywood movies. They are kind of wack but sometimes totally amazing! Dad was the one who got us into them. I told Aamir that, but now I'm afraid that saying it might have seemed dorky.

He asked why I called my grandmother "Bibi," and I explained that my father had been from Kenya and that "Bibi" was Swahili for "grandmother." He thanked me for the information.

Bibi herself, all stout and smiling, was waiting at the bus station.

She had come alone, which made me happy. I thought she might have her boyfriend, Herb, with her. Herb is all right, but I wanted Bibi to myself for a while!

On the minus side, she had to show photo ID before the Overlord of the Bus Terminal (that is, the driver) would release me to her. I know there are valid reasons for this. Even so, it was fairly humiliating.

Bibi was driving her pickup truck. The thing is plenty beat up, but I love it. We threw my bags into the bed, then I climbed into the cab and we headed for the farm. This required driving through town, which is a weird experience, since Vande Velde's Landing has an amazing number of yards crammed with garden-gnome statues. Well, I suppose it's no surprise if you consider that gnomes are the town's official tourist attraction. The gift shops sell all kinds of tacky gnome souvenirs, including a document called the Charter of the Gnome Protective Association. It's handwritten on brown parchment paper, and you can buy it framed or unframed.

I think all that might explain the crazy dream I had when I was so sick last summer. So much wacky gnome stuff probably put it into my head.

Soon enough we were out of town and jouncing along the back roads. I liked the way the truck bounced and rattled on this part of the trip. Something about that felt very real.

I've been here a couple of hours now and I'm a little worried about Bibi. She's as wonderful as ever, of course. And it was no surprise that she had a big batch of cookies ready for me. But though she's obviously happy to see me, she seems nervous and upset. I kept asking her about it, but she never gave me a straight answer.

What could be bothering her?

Despite that worry, I'm happy to be here. This afternoon I plan to go for a ramble in the woods. Bibi showed me the way around last year, so she doesn't worry when I go out there. I'll toss a book and a bottle of water in my backpack, and it will be great.

★   ★

The Charter of the Gnome Protective Association

❧ When in the course of human and nonhuman events, it becomes necessary for one people to shield another from discovery and persecution, then those of goodwill and stout heart must step forward to take a stand.

❧ That time has come for us in Vande Velde's Landing.

❧ The very name of our society is reflective of what this declaration is about. We now have among us a contingent of gnomes, tiny folk, intelligent and highly moral, who came here from the home country and need our assistance.

❧ Though our gnome neighbors are in large part self-sufficient, there are certain things they need from us and certain services they are willing to perform in return, as is appropriate in a good Dutch bargain.

❧ What they most desire, profoundly and intensely, is privacy and protection from prying eyes. Thus it is that we, certain elders in the village of Vande Velde's Landing, have gathered to pledge our aid and give our assurance of secrecy to these, our tiny but most worthy neighbors.

❧ The gnomes have vowed to provide similar aid to us as they are able—especially in medical matters, where they have great skill and knowledge.

⁂ With this charter we decree that we will do all in our power to shield our small neighbors from the prying eyes of the world. We will respect their privacy and give no sign or hint that such folk live among or near to us.

⁂ To this we pledge our sacred honor.

⁂ Furthermore, as the continuance of this promise and pledge is of utmost importance, we vow to bring into our membership only the most honorable and trustworthy of souls, generation to generation, so that this pact might go on forever.

⁂ Thus it is, thus may it ever be.

Signed July 12, 1732, by

Joost Metzen   *Frans Vande Velde*

Ursula Nickel   *Otto Ottman*

Magda Carlsen   *Gertrude Hoogendoorn*

Abram Hildebrandt   *Jacob Riddlehoover*

Elbert Rosencrantz   *Anna Shoopman*

Monday, June 29

I am leaving tonight and that's that!

After what happened today I can no longer stay. The humiliation is too great.

Oddly, the final push to send me out on my own did not come from Cyril and Violet and their relentless teasing.

It came from my father.

The only good thing I can say about this is that Dad did not intentionally hurt my feelings. It was only because I overheard him talking to Mom that this boiling pain is cascading across my heart.

I honestly did not plan to eavesdrop on my parents. It was just that when I came back to our cave to fetch my diary I heard them talking.

✦ ✦ ✦

Had to put down my feather for a little while, as I was too overcome with grief to continue. Little did I anticipate how agonizing it would be to write this entry!

Deep breath.

All right, here's what happened: Returning from sky ballet practice, I landed on the ledge outside our cave. Before I could enter, I heard my father exclaim, "Cecelia, I am so worried about Gerald that I am starting to molt!"

This hit me hard. Part of me wanted to flee, but even stronger was the desire to hear my parents' conversation.

Mom's first words were comforting. "Now, Reggie, let's not be overly concerned."

"I am not 'overly concerned'!" Dad shouted. "I am realistic. You know very well that in only two weeks Gerald has to add a treasure to his hoard. You know equally well that Cyril and Violet have already worked out what they want for their tenths, and how to obtain the treasures."

This was a surprise, and a distinctly upsetting one. Neither of my sibs had mentioned anything about this to me. I felt terribly left out.

"Do you have any sense that Gerald has even considered the problem?" continued Dad.

I wanted to shout, "Of course I've considered it! I think about it every day!"

Unfortunately, you shouldn't shout at someone you're eavesdropping on.

"Now, Reggie," said Mom. "Have some faith in the boy."

"Faith?" cried Dad (who has always had a powerful temper). "Give me one good reason to have faith!"

I waited for my mother to answer, but she remained silent.

Even she could not find a reason to give him hope!

As if her silence had not blasted my heart hard enough,

the next sound to come from the cave was a hammer blow to my heart.

My father began to weep!

"I had such hope for the boy," he sobbed. "He should have been first-hatched, first in my heart, first to take wing. But always he has hung back, always delayed, always been in fear. Always shamed me."

"Not always," said Mom gently. "There was the first hunting of the rabbits. He took the lead in that."

"They were *rabbits*!" exploded Dad. He let out a heavy sigh, then said, "Do you have any idea how hard it is for me to face the other fathers? They boast and brag of their children, especially their first-hatched, and their mighty deeds. When it should be my turn, all I can do is shrug my wings and say, 'Gerald has yet to come into his own.' Then I feel like a fool and wish I could slink back to our cave and hide."

It is one thing to endure the teasing of my siblings. It is another thing entirely to bring such pain to my father, whom I love more than I love the sky and flight itself.

It is indeed time for me to run (or fly) away.

Therefore, tonight is the night.

I must be as brave as Izzikiah Wildbeak in *The Griffinagria*. He is my hero, and I want to act as he would act.

How I wish I could write poems with the power and strength of the verse in *The Griffinagria*!

Here is my poem for today, the longest and saddest I have ever written:

Gerald the Griffin
Has let down his mother,
Also his father
And sister and brother.

Gerald feels lonely,
Gerald feels bad,
Gerald is sorry
He's made his dad sad.

Gerald is leaving,
Gerald can't stay,
Gerald is packing
And flying away!

I suppose that's kind of self-pitying, but it's the way I feel right now.

Besides, it's not for anyone else to read.

Clearly as a poet I still have a lot to learn. But here is the one thing I do know. Tonight I will be flying at full speed headfirst into a cliff.

If I do not survive, this will be my last entry.

The Griffinagria of Josiah Cloudclaws

*T*he Griffinagria is generally considered the greatest artistic achievement of the griffin world. Written by Josiah Cloudclaws approximately two thousand years ago, this epic poem chronicles in exquisite verse the origin of the griffins, their early years of struggle, and, most important, the leadership of Izzikiah Wildbeak in the great war with the Arimaspians.

Within this vast and wondrous work, which is filled with wisdom and adventure, can be found all the truths needed for a griffin to lead a good and proper life. Indeed, it is the source of the Code of the Griffins.

No aerie is complete without a copy of this magnificent epic. We now offer a gorgeous leather-bound edition, featuring over one hundred original illustrations, available for purchase from our offices in reasonable monthly installments.

PARENTS SHOULD NOT LET THEIR GRIFFLINGS ESCAPE THE AERIE WITHOUT READING THIS CORE TEXT!

So you'll know what <u>The Griffinagria</u> is like, here is a typical stanza.—G.O.

And in those days of rage did Izzikiah,
Who was, of griffins, greatest in all ways,
Spread wide his wings to cool rise of a fire

That if not quenched might set the world ablaze.
But, O! the price he paid for his harsh blow
Would haunt the high-flown warrior all his days.

For his own child, who caused his heart to glow
(Egg-born, first-hatched, his image on the wing),
Now deep into forbidden realms needs go.

And from those dark and fearful haunts must bring
Sweet balm to soothe the broken heart's sharp sting.

Did you catch the rhyme structure? It's ABA, BCB, CDC, DD. Unfortunately, it's a bit weak in the first stanza ("Izzikiah" and "fire") due to translation issues.

Anyway, this is called terza rima, and we griffins taught it to the Italian poet Dante, who used it as the form for his <u>Divine Comedy.</u> Speaking for myself, I would give two talons and several pinfeathers to be able to write like this!—G.O.

Tuesday, June 30

So much to write about since my last entry!

To be painfully honest (and why should I be anything but honest in my own diary?), I must start with this: Despite my vow to leave last night, I once again backed away from the idea.

This was *not* mere cowardice. It was the realization that I had no idea *which* stone walls might be "designated points of passage"! The idea of running (flying) away felt simple when it first came to me. That was because back then I had no idea how dangerous it would be to attempt to leave the Enchanted Realm!

I was trying to sleep but not having much success. Just as I did finally start to drift off, I was pulled back to wake-fulness by a tug on one of my ears!

It was Master Abelard. He was sitting on my head, his favorite place for delivering instruction. Speaking softly into my right ear he said, "Gerald, I know you have been thinking about running away."

"How could you know that?" I yelped.

"Not so loud! Get up and slink out onto the ledge so we can talk."

I did as he ordered, using the "thistledown on the

breeze" technique Dad taught us when we were first learning to hunt.

It was a clear night, illumined by a bright half-moon. The air was cool and crisp. The canyon that stretches so deep below the ledge was mostly in shadow.

Once we were safely away from my sleeping family, I repeated softly, "How did you know I was thinking about running away?"

"Because I know *you*, Gerald. I understand the way you think, even if you don't always understand it yourself. If you truly want to go, I am ready to accompany you. I believe I can give you considerable help with life on the other side of the Transcendental Curtain."

This was such a remarkable statement that I could barely contain a squawk.

"You'll come with me?" I asked, voice low as I was able.

"Yes. The fact is, I need to get away from the university for a while. And, as your tutor, I feel this journey will be a good way to continue your education."

I took a deep breath, then admitted my fears. "Master A, I read an article on how to enter the human world. I don't know where there is a cave or tree that will work, and I don't think I can do that flying-straight-into-a-stone-wall thing!"

"I can help you with that," he said.

I felt a huge sense of relief. "You mean you know where there's a cave we can go through?"

"No. But I do know where there's a Wall of Passage. And I will be with you to encourage you, to keep you believing that you can fly through it. So we should be fine."

Trying not to cry, I said, "I don't think I can do it!"

He gave my ear a sharp tug. "Nonsense! Here is how much I believe in you. I will ride on your beak as we fly toward the stone wall! That way, if you fail, which I do *not* think will happen, I will be the first to smash into it!"

The thought that my teacher had so much faith in me that he would risk his life believing in my own faith brought a tear to my eye. "You really think I can do it?" I asked.

"No, I'm just looking for a fast way to die!"

As I've noted, Master A can be quite sarcastic.

"I can't go without my hoard," I said, partly because it was true, partly to change the subject and buy some time.

"I know that. It's why I gave you that pack last month when I realized you were thinking about doing this. Everything is already stored in it, right?"

"Yes."

"Then quietly bring it out here. I'll help you strap it on."

Getting the pack properly situated turned out to be more complicated than Master A seemed to have expected.

"I think you've grown," he complained, while trying to pull the straps tight.

Secretly, I hoped he might not be able to manage it, as that would give me an excuse not to do this after all. Much as I hate to admit it, even to myself, I was still not entirely ready to go.

Why am I always wanting to do something and at the same time *not* wanting to do it? Is it true, as Master Abelard has told me so many times, that being both eagle and lion has given me a divided nature?

Even if it is true, should not both halves of my nature be bold and fearless?

✦　✦　✦

Back to what actually happened. Once Master A managed to get the travel pouch strapped into place, he said, "Everything ready, steady, and ready. Let's go!"

"I can't go yet," I answered.

"Why not?" he asked, and I could tell he was getting impatient.

"Because I have to leave a note!"

Master A sighed. He has a wide variety of very expressive sighs, and this was one I knew well. It meant that despite the fact that he didn't like what I said, he accepted that I was right. He lowered himself into my travel pouch, then lifted up my bottle of ink. I took it from his hands. Next he tore a page from the back of my diary and handed it up to me.

I flinched when he did that, but it was true that I had nothing else on which to leave my note, which I wrote by the light of the moon.

Dear Family,

I have gone to seek my future.

Please do not look for me. I will return if ever the time comes when I can look Dad in the eye and feel he will no longer think me a disgrace to our aerie.

I love you all, despite the way you have treated me. May the Great Griffin keep you in the shelter of his wings.

Your son and/or sibling,
Gerald

Tuesday, June 30 (continued)

As soon as I had secured the note under a rock, Master Abelard said, "Let's fly!"

I knelt so he could climb to the top of my head. Once he was in place and clinging to my right ear, I could delay no longer. I backed into the mouth of the cave . . . then raced forward and launched into the air.

Instantly we were soaring above the deep abyss that yawns below my family's aerie.

I do not often fly by moonlight, mostly because Mom does not approve. But truly it is one of the most beautiful things you can do . . . especially if you are in the mountains. The rich silver light highlights the tors and crags and makes mysteries of the valleys and crevices. My mind itched at the thought that *anything* could be hidden in those dark and mysterious places. After all, we were in the Enchanted Realm! Another time I would have contemplated what monsters and wonders might have been waiting there.

Not now, though.

This night I was a griffin on a mission!

"Head toward the Shanamal Valley," ordered Master Abelard.

I banked to the right.

The flying was easy, the winds and updrafts holding me so firmly I could glide much of the way. I barely needed to work my wings; mostly I used them to steer, tilting first left and then right as I careened between the rocky crags.

If the flight at that point was easy, my mind was anything but at ease.

All I could think about was the great test that lay ahead.

Could I really make it through the wall?

Master Abelard, who was clinging to my right ear, suddenly leaned into it and shouted, "Turn here! Fly past that outcropping."

I did as he ordered. A moment later he cried, "There's our cliff, about three hundred feet ahead!"

My heart grew soft and fearful, and my stomach clenched with dread.

"Glide for a moment while I position myself on your beak," said Master Abelard.

This made me feel a little better, as it told me he truly did believe I could fly straight through that solid wall of rock!

Climbing down my face, my teacher positioned himself flat upon my beak, then placed one small hand in each of my nostrils.

I knew this was so he would not fall off. I just hoped it wouldn't make me sneeze!

Once firmly situated, he cried, "Now fly, Gerald! *FLY!*"

Stretching my wings to their fullest, I flapped with all

my might. At the same time I whispered to myself, "I think I can, I think I can, I think I can! I *know* I can!"

I was flying full-speed. We were mere feet from the cliff. I wanted to close my eyes but feared if I did it would indicate I didn't really believe I would make it through . . . and thus would crash and die. Worse, it wouldn't be just me who would die. If I didn't make it, I would kill my teacher, who was staking his life on his belief in me!

"Faster, Gerald!" cried Master Abelard. "Don't stop believing!"

I flew on, gaining speed with each stroke of my wings.

The cliff loomed before us.

Would we collide and die or glide right through to the human world?

I must not question. I had to believe!

✦　✦　✦

That's all I can write for now. I'm tired and my words are starting to wobble.

From: Huntsline Airfield
Date: June 30
Time: 01:10
To: Federal Aviation Administration
Re: Unidentified Aircraft

At 23:15 hours last night a small aircraft appeared on our radar screen. (One observer insists we should refer to it as an unidentified flying object, but I refuse to indulge in such nonsense.)

After repeated attempts to contact the aircraft met with no success, several drones were sent out, ready to shoot down the intruding aircraft if necessary. Some laser blasts were fired. However, storm conditions made visual tracking via the drones nearly impossible.

At 23:25 the unidentified aircraft fell below radar-detection levels.

We have been monitoring all channels for word of a crash, but nothing has come in.

No further information available at this time.

                    Respectfully submitted,
                    Rodney Parker
                    Airman First Class

Tuesday, June 30 (continued)

All right, I've recovered a bit, so I can write more now. I do want to get all this down while it is fresh in my memory.

So . . . when we were a few feet from the cliff I did close my eyes. Actually my eyes closed themselves. I couldn't stop them!

According to Master Abelard, I also emitted a shriek of terror.

To be honest, I think he did, too.

There was no halting at that point, of course, no turning aside. The collision was unavoidable.

I braced myself for the impact, which indicated I did not believe. But maybe I had believed enough already, because I didn't feel any sudden crash against stone, didn't feel any pain, didn't feel . . . anything.

I wondered if this meant that I was now dead.

Then Master Abelard cried, "You did it, Gerald! You did it!"

I opened my eyes and saw that the terrain below was entirely different from the land I had been flying over moments earlier.

We were in the human world!

"But I didn't feel anything," I said.

"You weren't supposed to," shouted Master A as he

crawled back toward the top of my head. He sounded calm, but once he had positioned himself and was holding on to my ear I could feel him tremble.

Had *he* not believed we were going to make it through?

By the light of the moon, nearly as bright in the human world as it had been in the Enchanted Realm, I could see that the landscape stretching below was more gentle than that of home. Oh, we were still flying over mountains. But unlike the bare and rocky peaks of home, these mountains were low and round and covered with trees.

I tried to spot a place to land so I could recover from our passage. The problem was not that my wings were tired. It was that my *heart* was totally wrung out by fear!

However, the dense forest presented a problem. The upper branches of the trees certainly could not hold my weight. And they grew so close together that I could see no opening through which I could reach the ground.

Adding to the problem, a stiff wind made it hard to keep a steady course. The sky was heavy with scudding clouds, which soon blocked the moon, plunging this new world into complete blackness . . . a blackness broken when somewhere ahead a bolt of lightning streaked down. Its hot white crackle was followed so quickly by a rumble of thunder that I knew it had been terribly close.

"Gerald, we have to land!" cried Master Abelard. "I'm having a hard time holding on in this wind."

He had to shout to be heard above the gusts, even though he had thrust his head directly *into* my ear!

"I can't see anyplace to touch down!" I shouted back.

Another bolt of lightning sliced the air to our right.

"Turn a bit to the left," bellowed Master A.

At that moment the rain started.

I do not like to fly in the rain!

To make things worse, we heard a noise from behind. Before I could turn my head to see what it was, a bolt of green light flashed past us! The light was straight and narrow, not jagged like lightning. And it traveled sideways rather than up and down.

"What was that?" I cried.

Instead of answering, Master A tightened his grip on my ear and shrieked, "Lasers! Dive, Gerald! Dive if you want to live to see the morning!"

I dove.

"Get as close to the trees as you can! Go lower. *Lower!*"

I was terrified. Had someone pursued us through the Transcendental Curtain? Were we about to be arrested?

Another bolt of green light shot past, followed almost instantly by another flare of real lightning up ahead. In its brief brilliance I spotted a gap in the trees! It was miles away (given my eagle eyes, I have amazing vision) but exactly what we needed.

Picking up speed, fighting the wind, barely skimming the treetops, I raced for the gap.

The rain drove against us, hard as pebbles. The wind knocked me first right, then left, as if it could not make up its mind which direction it was blowing from. I was in constant danger of being slammed into the treetops.

"Hold tight, teacher!" I bellowed, terrified one of the gusts might blow Master A off my head and send him tumbling into the darkness.

As we drew closer to the open space I had spotted, I saw that it had buildings!

I felt a new wave of dismay. Buildings meant people, which meant there was a chance we would be spotted by humans!

How many ways can I violate the Great Code before Izzikiah Wildbeak himself comes back from the dead and strikes me down for my sins?

"We'll take shelter in that barn!" shouted Master Abelard.

Hoping the wind would not swallow my words, I cried, "Someone might see us!"

"No one will be out in this storm, Gerald. Get us down and we'll hide there for the night."

I landed directly in front of the barn, splashing into a puddle as I did.

I was exhausted, sodden, thoroughly miserable.

Happily, we had one piece of good fortune . . . the barn doors were open.

"Hurry inside!" shouted Master A. "I want to get out of this gnome-drenching downpour!"

I did as he ordered, still nervous about being spotted.

It was pitch-black inside the building but totally dry. So that was one small comfort.

"Unless some tramp has taken shelter here for the night, I think it's safe to say there are no humans nearby," Master Abelard said. "There may be some livestock, but they won't bother us."

"I can't see a thing!" I complained. (I may have amazing vision, but I need *some* light to move around.)

"Give me a moment," replied Master A.

I don't know what he did, other than mutter a few words I couldn't understand, but seconds later light was streaming from the top of my head! Well, not actually *from* my head. At least I think not. That's just where Master Abelard was sitting. Something he had done was causing the light.

Strange as this was, I was grateful to have him with me. He is so much wiser than me and knows so much more about the human world. For example: For reasons I was not able to understand, he said, "Clearly not a working barn. So much the better. Head to your right, Gerald."

I moved as he directed, winding my way through large and complicated chunks of metal, one of which he called a "tractor." Soon we came to two long sticks. About a dozen shorter sticks, evenly spaced, went crosswise between them.

"This is a ladder," said Master A. "It's for climbing."

I prefer climbing rocks, or flying, but I slowly made my way up the rickety thing. It trembled beneath me, which was scary. If it broke there would be no time—or room!—to spread my wings and fly.

At the top of the ladder I was forced to tuck my wings against my sides in order to squeeze through a hole. We found ourselves in what Master A called a loft. It was a wide space, completely empty, bounded by wooden walls. The wall to our left had a set of what my teacher informed me were stairs. I climbed them (easier to use than the ladder) and found a second loft. This one contained a great deal of loose straw.

I arranged some into a pile to make a nesting place. Wobbling from weariness, I settled into it. Master Abelard nestled against my side, tucking himself under the covering of my wing.

Outside, the storm continued to rage; inside the barn, which was like a giant wooden cave, we were safe and dry.

I fell into a deep sleep.

When I woke this morning my illusions of safety were shattered.

Master Abelard had vanished!

Panic-stricken, I flung the straw about, digging at it frantically with my talons. Where was he? What could have happened to him? I could not help myself. I let out a wail of despair.

"For the love of all that's enchanted, be quiet!" cried Master A. "Someone might hear you!"

"Where are you?" I called, too relieved to care how cranky he had sounded. "Are you all right?"

"I'm fine, Gerald. I'm over here in the storage area. I was just trying to see if I could find anything interesting."

I sank down and crossed my talons over my face.

Sometimes I am such an idiot!

(Summer Assignment)

6/30 (Tues.)

We had a very big storm last night. There was a lot of thunder. I was afraid lightning would hit the barn.

I can see the barn from my room. It is huge. It would be a good place for a clubhouse, but I would need friends for that.

We do not have Internet here. I guess I will just have to read some books. That should make my teachers happy.

(3 paragraphs, 3 sentences each, 1 of them compound.)

6/30

Holy melting marshmallows! When I went up to the attic to poke around this morning, two things happened . . . one kind of strange, the other actually bloodcurdling. I should start with a little about the attic. One of the many things I love about it is that it has its own special smell— old, musty, and kind of mysterious.

And it is crammed with STUFF! It would seriously take days to examine everything stored there. It's a massive collection of broken lamps, old clothes, birdcages, books, discarded board games, mysterious-looking trunks, and things I don't even have words for.

Most of the trunks have flat tops. Those have stacks of boxes on them, as does pretty much any flat surface up there. So you have to move stuff around if you want to look inside them. Some of the older trunks have rounded tops. I don't know why, but somehow that makes me really want to look inside them.

Standing against one wall is a rickety bookcase filled with really old books. Some are massively boring—things like *Minutes of the Vande Velde's Landing Town Meetings for 1897.* I suppose somebody studying local history might think they were real treasures, but I can't imagine anyone else finding them interesting. Others are totally cool adventure stories written a hundred or more years ago.

You have to adjust your brain to read them, but once you do the stories are great!

It was while I was looking at the books that I experienced the bloodcurdling moment I mentioned. I was at the back of the attic, which faces the barn. From the barn I heard—*distinctly* heard—a screech that sounded like some creature in a state of terror.

I froze in place, but the sound stopped almost immediately and didn't start again.

What could it have been?

After several minutes of silence I went back to exploring the attic. I found a big stash of old jigsaw puzzles and pulled out a couple to take downstairs. Bibi and I like to work on puzzles on rainy days or nights when we just feel like staying up late and talking. We chat while we're trying to find the pieces we want. Sometimes Bibi tells me stories from when she was young.

It was shortly after I found the puzzles that I made the *big* discovery. It happened when I opened an old trunk. The first thing I saw was a faded brown blanket. I was afraid the whole thing would be filled with sheets and boring stuff like that. I almost closed it right then but decided to dig a little deeper. So I lifted out the blanket.

Underneath it I found a stack of paintings.

Paintings of gnomes.

These weren't paintings of those little garden statues, though. These were realistic paintings, with the gnomes sitting in cozy homes, or talking to rabbits, or playing games. One showed a whole family of gnomes riding on a raccoon.

I added one of the pictures to my stack of puzzles and took it down to show Bibi. She looked startled and a little uncomfortable when she saw it.

"That was done by your great-uncle Lukas," she said.

She sounded flustered. When I asked why, she said, "Well, he shouldn't have painted them."

Which I thought was a very odd answer.

"How come no one ever mentioned this uncle to me before?" I asked.

"Oh, he's been gone for years, dear. Now come with me. We need to go outside and check the garden to see if last night's storm did any damage. It was a real toad strangler."

Clearly she was trying to change the subject.

WHY??

From the Notebook of Abelard Chronicus

◇◇◇◇◇◇◇◇◇◇◇◇◇◇◇◇◇◇◇◇

June 30

We have landed in just the place I was hoping for! The storm was helpful in that regard, as it gave me a good reason to direct Gerald toward the Riddlehoover farm.

On the other hand, the attack by the human planes was unnerving. I had not been anticipating that!

Of course, the only reason I knew what those things were was because of my "forbidden" research, which has led me to understand far more about the human world than I really wanted to. But without that research, Gerald and I might have died last night. So, I wave my beard at "forbidden" research. It is an idea for small hearts and tight digestive systems!

On the plus side, every fiber of my being is whispering that what I have come here in search of, what I have been after all these years, is close by.

I have to be right. I HAVE TO BE! Otherwise all my research, all the years of scorn, not to mention the shameful way I have used Gerald . . . all of that will be for nothing.

Feh.

My "feelings" are slender threads to put my trust in. Better to rely on the books, the research, the interpretation, the reading between the lines, the leaps of instinct driven by fact and discovery. We are not far from my goal, and I am close to finding that which was lost to me.

I would bet my life on it.

For that matter, I *have* bet my life on it.

And maybe Gerald's as well.

The griffling is asleep now, a well-earned rest. I know the flight toward and through the stone wall was emotionally exhausting for him. Why didn't I have the courage to be honest with him about that? Given how many other rules and laws I am breaking, you would think I could have broken that one, too.

I guess there is truth in the saying that old habits die hard. My habit of secrecy still shapes my behavior.

One more reason to feel ashamed.

Tuesday, June 30 (continued)

After my cry of despair Master Abelard came strolling across the wooden floor as if nothing at all had happened. But his words were harsh on my heart. Looking up at me, he said, "Gerald, you must stop reacting to every moment of worry as if it were the greatest terror you have ever experienced. I am right here. I woke up early. I did some exploring. I found some fascinating things."

"Like what?" I replied, hoping a sign of interest would reduce some of the way I had humiliated myself.

But all he said was "I prefer not to discuss that now. The most pressing issue at the moment is how to feed you."

He was right about that. My stomach was empty and I needed to hunt. But how could I do that? It was broad daylight and we were in the human world. I could not allow myself to be seen! Happily, his words gave me hope.

"You know a place where I can get food right now?" I asked eagerly.

Master A shook his head. "No. You're going to have to wait until nightfall. I just mean we need to think about the best way for you to leave the barn without being seen when the time comes."

"I can't wait until night!" I replied, trying not to whine. "I am hungry *now!*"

Not only was I hungry, I was annoyed. That's because I hadn't been thinking about how hungry I was until Master A mentioned the topic.

I also felt stupid, because back when I decided to run away I hadn't even thought about the matter of eating.

Still, given the terrain we flew over last night, it shouldn't be a problem. The area is just right for my favorite foods, fish and bunnies.

Bunnies especially. They are tasty-good balls of furry yumbo!

Especially the pink ones.

Here is today's poem:

Bunnies are yummy,
Bunnies are great.
I wish that I had some
Right now on my plate.

Phooey. The rhymes are good, but since griffins don't use plates, it doesn't quite make sense.

Poems should make sense, right?

I was pulled from thoughts of plates, food, and poems by Master A snapping, "If you hadn't slept so late, we could have gotten out of this barn while it was still dark." He closed his eyes, pinched the bridge of his nose, took a deep breath, then said, "I'm sorry, Gerald. That was unfair. You flew a mighty flight last night. It's just that I am on edge right now."

That is one of the things I love about my teacher. He is willing to admit when he has been unnecessarily harsh.

That still didn't solve the problem of me being hungry.

Or the problem that the only possible meal anywhere near me at that moment was Master A himself.

It always disturbs me when I am so hungry I begin thinking about the fact that I could swallow him with a single bite.

I began counting pieces of straw to distract myself.

From the Notebook of Abelard Chronicus

◇◇◇◇◇◇◇◇◇◇◇◇◇◇◇◇◇◇◇◇◇◇

June 30 (later)

It was never my intent to become a babysitter for a griffling. However, that seems to be my situation right now and I need to do it well, since Gerald is large and hungry, and I am small and edible.

I am torn between caring for my charge and charging off to follow my own mission.

Were it not for my wretched conscience, I would have been long gone by now.

Would that I could be the scoundrel I like to imagine myself to be!

I blame my inability to be properly ruthless on my mother.

Mom

Tuesday, June 30 (early evening)

I'm so hungry that I could eat a dragon's butt, scales and all!

If I do not get something to eat soon I fear Master A will be in trouble.

Gaaah! How can I even think such a thing?

I am no mere beast!

I am a griffin, proud and fierce!

But I hunger. . . .

From the Notebook of Abelard Chronicus

◇◇◇◇◇◇◇◇◇◇◇◇◇◇◇◇◇◇◇◇

June 30 (evening)

Darkness arrived just in time and I was able to direct Gerald to the woods, where he could hunt. I am not sure how much longer he could have restrained his appetite.

Now that he is gone, I can leave to pursue my own quest.

I plan to be back before morning, of course.

It would not be good to leave the griffling on his own.

7/1

By the Great Googly Pasta Monster, I swear I am as fascinated by Bibi's barn as I am by her attic.

Unfortunately, the place also creeps me out. It's so old and rickety that when I'm in there I get the feeling the whole thing might collapse on my head at any moment.

That's not just my "overactive imagination" (thank you, school shrink) at work. I've seen collapsed barns while Bibi and I have driven around on errands. They make me shudder.

And then, of course, there's what happened to Dad . . .

Despite these things, the barn still fascinates me. Or maybe it's because of them? (Again, thank you, school shrink.) Well, all that aside, I love the abandoned farm equipment (fun to climb on!). I love the tool bench. I love that at the back of the ground floor a ladder leads to the loft—two lofts, actually. The lower loft is empty, the upper loft still has some straw and (even better) a storage area with a collection of stuff almost as cool as what's in Bibi's attic.

I guess my antecedents had too much junk to keep in one place.

Mmmmmm—I smell bacon! (Bibi feeds me much better than Mom does.) Need to finish this up so I can go down to breakfast. But later today I plan to check out the barn.

By "later" I mean sometime around noon, when the sun

is high and bright and I am less likely to run into something that might, as Bibi likes to say, "go bump in the night."

Actually she has a whole poem about things that go bump in the night. She says it came from Scotland, where I guess we had two or three ancestors about a billion years ago. Sometimes I ask her to say the poem to me just before I go to bed. She gets a gleam in her eye, puts on a Scottish accent, and recites:

From ghoulies and ghosties
And long-leggedy beasties
And things that go bump in the night,
Good Lord, deliver us!

✦   ✦   ✦

Of course, I don't really think there's anything crazy-weird out in the barn.

Not really.

Seriously, not really!

Even so, I'm not going out there until sometime around noon.

In other news, Bibi's friend Herb is coming for dinner tonight. That's all right. I like him well enough, despite his corny jokes.

Or maybe because of them.

I just wish he wouldn't try to talk to me about Dad.

Letter and photo from Bradley Ashango's desk drawer

Brad—

Hey, son! How you doing? I'm okay, except for the fact that I miss you and your mom so much. The work here is going well. I feel like I'm really doing some good for these folks.

And here's some other good news: I should be home at the end of July! We'll have some times then, eh, my lad? For one thing, we can get back to that book we've been working on. I can't wait to see what we cook up next for our poor hero!

Hope the heat isn't getting to you—I know what summer in the city can be like.

Love always to you and your mom,

Dad

PS: I'm enclosing a picture of me. One of my buddies at the clinic took this. He actually has an old-fashioned camera that uses film!

Wednesday, July 1

Last night I hunted, and I fed, and that was good.

The fact that bunnies exist in both the Enchanted Realm and the human world is proof that the Great Griffin loves us!

When I returned from my hunt, Master Abelard was not in the barn.

I did not worry. . . . I assumed he had gone out to forage himself. Remembering how he had chastised me when I panicked the first time I thought he was gone, I told myself that all was well.

Tired from the work of hunting, I slept.

To my horror, when I woke this morning he still was not here!

New panic rose within me.

I tried to fight it back, but I am lost without him.

Where can he be?

Has some dread catastrophe befallen him?

What will I do without his guidance?

I am a griffin alone, a stranded soul, a stranger in a strange land!

I wonder if my family is thinking about me now. Do they miss me? Worry about me? Or are they just glad that I'm gone?

I wish I had a little bird that could tell me, that could watch them and report back.

Wait! I just heard something.

Must stop writing . . . I need to be ready for anything.

OMG!

OMG OMG OMG!

OMG!

Wednesday, July 1 (continued)

I have been seen.
I have been seen!!!
I have violated—no, shattered!—the Great Code of
the Griffins.
I am a horrible griffin.
I despair.

NEW BATAVIA TOWN CRIER

JULY 1

LOST CITIZEN RECOVERED FROM THE WOODS!

By Marta Joosten

Last night one of the Up Above patrols came across a gnome, wounded and insensible, lying half-hidden beneath a fallen fern. Had he not emitted a moan as they were passing by, the patrol might not have discovered him at all. (The consequences should a human have found him are too horrifying to contemplate.)

It turned out to be the well-known alarmist Eduard Chronicus. The patrol carried him back underground with them, and he is now resting in the Level One hospital.

Attempts to question him about what happened have been put off until he has had time to recover.

From art on file

7/1

I am not crazy.

Seriously, I do not think I am crazy.

Except maybe I am.

Because I just saw a griffin in the barn.

I mean, gnomes are one thing. But a freaking GRIFFIN?!

This CANNOT be real.

But what if it is?!?!

Wednesday, July 1 (later)

My heart is fluttering like a startled bird. That is not entirely weird—I am part bird after all. But that bird part is all eagle, and I should not be affrighted by a mere human. Well, I wasn't really frightened by the human itself. It's having been seen that is causing me to panic.

Here is what happened. When I heard that sound, I set aside my diary and moved into pounce stance, ready to fight if need be. Gazing ahead with an eagle eye, I saw the face of a human peering at me from the stairs that lead to this part of the loft. It was a boy, I think (I have no experience with humans, so it is hard to be sure). When our eyes met he let out a gasp, then scrambled down and away.

Oh, I am a bad, bad griffin to have let myself be seen!

I am surprised I have not already been blasted by a bolt of sacred lightning.

And what should I do now? Fly back to the Enchanted Realm? Great Izzikiah! I suddenly realize I do not even know how to do that! I had counted on Master A to help me when (if ever) it was time to return.

Even if I did know how, I couldn't go without him.

I am not such a bad griffin that I would abandon my teacher.

But what has happened to him?

What if he is sick, or injured, or even (the feather trembles in my talons as I write this) . . . dead?

I don't know what to do!

From the Notebook of Abelard Chronicus

◇◇◇◇◇◇◇◇◇◇◇◇◇◇◇◇◇◇◇◇

July 1

I have achieved my goal! However, I have done it in a most backward way. Instead of finding an entrance to Batavia, I was carried here while unconscious.

Here is what happened. I was at the edge of the forest, searching for some sign of the city, when I was snatched up by an owl!

I should have been watching for owls, but years of living in the Enchanted Realm, where we have a pact of peace with them, had made me incautious. During that heart-stopping moment when I was snatched from the ground, I cursed myself for the carelessness that I knew could cost me my life. I also knew that I had to act fast or end up as nothing more than an owl pellet!

Fortunately, my captor had made an awkward grab and I had one arm free. Drawing my knife, I stabbed at his foot. I knew if he let me go, the plunge to earth might kill me. But to remain in his clutches was certain death, whereas I am small enough and light enough that there was at least a chance I could survive the fall.

Three quick jabs was all it took. The bird screeched in rage but opened his talons.

I plummeted downward, bounced off a branch, then another, then another . . . and that's the last thing I remember until I woke here in New Batavia, as it's now called. So my calculations and research were right. If only I could tell Henrik!

I am in a hospital of some sort. My head hurts, my left arm is in a sling, and I have a serious puncture wound in my side from one of the owl's talons.

If not for the quality of gnomic medicine, I might not have made it through the night!

I am being treated well, but they have mistaken me for someone else . . . a fact that fills me with both joy and dread. Joy because it means the one I seek is known here. Dread because he himself must be missing. Otherwise why would they think I am him?

Someone is coming. Will write more later.

7/1 (continued)

I'm feeling calmer now, so I think I can manage to write down what happened a little while ago . . . even though it's as weird as deep-fried cauliflower in peanut butter sauce. (Which my mother actually tried to feed me one night!)

Deep breath. Okay, here goes. As I had planned, I went out to the barn after lunch. The sky was bright and clear, so it seemed about as safe as it could ever be . . . after all, nothing can go "bump in the night" when it's the middle of the day! To be honest, I didn't really think there was anything out there anyway. Mostly I wanted to examine the place as a possible spot to hang out. Assuming I can find someone around here to be friends with, it might make a good clubhouse.

I started by poking around on the ground floor. I climbed on the old tractor (which I am hoping Bibi will teach me to drive this year). Then I studied the circular saw blades that hang on the wall; they would be great for that horror vid I want to do someday, the one Dad and I wrote some scenes for.

Next I did what I always do and put my finger in the vise bolted to the old workbench. I know that sounds kind of stupid, but I like to pretend it's a medieval torture device and I want to see how much I can endure. I would love to think that if the evil minions of the king used it on me, I could keep from blurting out the vital secret that was key to the rebellion. Unfortunately, as soon as I actually start to tighten the vise, I know if someone did this to me for real I would crack faster than a walnut hit by a sledgehammer. Secrets would come flying out of my mouth like bats from a cave at twilight!

I looked around a little more but didn't find anything unusual. Then I climbed the ladder to the first loft. It stretches the width of the barn, a distance of about fifty feet. (I know because I paced it off one day last year.) It's empty and has no walls to divide it up, so the floor area seems huge.

Since there was no place for anything to hide, it was easy to see that there was nothing weird here. But as I was about to climb the steps to the next level, I heard a soft sound from above me.

I turned to run, then stopped and said to myself, "Don't be a derp. It's just the wind!"

I started up the steps. Even though I had told myself it was just the wind, I went slowly, ready to leap down and do the Big Scramboolian if I needed to. On the fourth step I leaned forward and pressed myself to the stairs, then lifted my eyes over the edge of the next level's floor.

Holy bouncing green tomatoes! I was looking at a griffin!

A freaking griffin!!!

I am not making this up, not imagining it, not playing a

game. I know what a griffin looks like. I haven't spent all that time reading myths and legends for nothing. This was the real thing . . . an enormous eaglelike head (with those doofy horse ears), massive wings folded along its sides, and the tawny body of a lion. It was bigger than a lion, though . . . more like a good-sized pony.

I was still gawping when it turned its gaze in my direction, looked me right in the eye, then let out a loud *GAAAH!*

Now I knew what I had heard yesterday! But there wasn't much satisfaction in that, since I was afraid the creature was about to leap forward and bite off my head. Heart pounding, I scrambled down the steps, down the ladder, and out of the barn, half expecting the griffin to come rushing after me.

It didn't.

In fact, I didn't hear any sound at all, other than myself gasping for breath.

But I know I didn't imagine it! The thing was too big, too solid, too real.

I don't know what to do now. The fact that it didn't chase me makes me wonder if it's not really dangerous. What if it's wounded or something and needs help?

I kind of want to go up there with my cell phone and see if I can get a picture of the thing, since no one will believe me if I just tell them about it. But somehow that seems wrong. I feel like I was given the chance to see something sacred and strange, something that didn't want to be seen, and I shouldn't talk about it, shouldn't spread it around.

Also, if anyone found out a griffin was here, they would want to capture it. That idea horrifies me.

I've decided not to tell Bibi about this, at least not yet. I know how it would go . . . most likely she would humor me, pretending to go along with some game I was playing, which would make me crazy. But there's a small chance she might decide to go out and look for herself. What if the creature really is dangerous and doesn't want an adult to see it? I can't put Bibi in danger that way!

Wednesday, July 1 (even later)

I am paralyzed by fear. It's broad daylight, so I can't flee the barn. If I did, I would be seen by even more people!

Besides, if I flee and Master Abelard returns, as I so fervently hope, how would he find me?

Even worse, what if I were to be captured?

No, that could never happen. I would just fly away!

But what if I couldn't? What if there are humans with nets out there right now, and they sent the boy to tempt me out?

Oh, where is Master A? And why in the world did I ever decide to run away?!

I have been crouching here for hours. But I have settled on what I will do if the boy comes back. My plan might be madness. It might be folly. But I am determined to carry through on it. After all, I can hardly make things worse.

Now that I've made a decision, I feel easier of mind.

Of course, it depends on the boy returning.

Which he might not do.

7/1 (continued)

Holy naked nectarines!

I'm so excited I can barely stay in my skin! But I have to write this all down, to be sure I'll remember it precisely.

So . . . after a few hours here in the house, I decided to go back to the barn. Part of me was terrified, of course. But seriously, how could I not check this out?

I climbed the ladder to the first loft, moving as silently as I could. Then, sticking close to the wall, I crawled over to the stairs that lead to the upper loft. I kind of snaked my way up them, then raised my head just high enough to peek over the edge.

The griffin was there . . . and he was looking right at me!

I slid down, terrified.

The griffin didn't attack. Instead, it called, "You can come back up if you want. I won't hurt you."

I hadn't been expecting that! But if a parrot can talk, then I guess there isn't any reason an eagle-headed creature can't do the same. Especially if it's a mythical being to begin with.

"Did you hear me?" it asked.

"Yes, but how do I know I can *believe* that you won't hurt me?"

"If I wanted to hurt you, I would have done it already!"

That made sense. The creature had to be very fast. He could have pounced on me before I made it halfway across the floor.

I took a deep breath, then climbed the steps. But I didn't go all the way up. Once my head was above the upper loft's floor level I stopped and said, "Promise you won't hurt me?"

"I am a civilized being," the griffin replied, sounding offended. "I would never eat a person. What I mostly like is fish and bunnies. So you're safe, and I'm pleased to meet you. Well, not entirely pleased, because I'm not supposed to be seen by humans at all. But mostly pleased, because I am lonely and frightened. Sorry, I'm dithering. I do that a lot." He stopped, took a breath, then said, "My name is Gerald."

"I'm Bradley," I answered, "and I am mostly pleased to meet you, too. Actually, as long as you're not going to eat me, I'm enormously pleased!"

"I would stand to greet you," said the griffin, "but I fear it might alarm you. So I will remain seated for now."

"Thank you, Gerald. I think I will also remain where I am for now." Trying to think of what to say next, I asked, "If you're not supposed to be seen by humans, why are you here?"

To my horror, he began to cry! Not loud sobs, just big tears that slowly rolled out of his eyes and down his enormous beak.

"I ran away from home. My teacher, Master Abelard, came with me, but he's disappeared, and I don't know what to do! I'm very frightened. It was very bad for me to let myself be seen by a human. I am afraid I will get in a lot of trouble for it."

Which was when I realized this griffin was really just a kid like me. I wanted to go pat him on the shoulder and tell him everything would be all right, but I wasn't ready to get that close. So I just said, "That must be very frightening for you. Where is your home?"

Gerald shrugged his wings. "Oh, around here somewhere."

"Do you mean you live right here in the Catskills?"

"No, no. I live in the Enchanted Realm. I say 'around here somewhere' because the Realm is connected to the human world. It's hard to explain. Think of it as the world next door. We're separated by a thing called the Transcendental Curtain. I came through the curtain not far from here."

He shuddered, and I could tell it had been a difficult journey.

"The thing is," he continued, "now that I'm in your world, home might as well be a million miles away, because I don't know how to go back!" His wings slumped and he wailed, "I can't go back anyway! I've done such a bad thing."

I was beginning to think Gerald was awfully high-strung for a griffin. I would have expected more boldness, and maybe less emotion.

He shook himself, then said, "Why don't you come up here? It will be easier to talk."

"I'm fine where I am," I answered, still not feeling entirely safe.

"So you're just going to stand on the stair and stare?" he asked.

I laughed. "I didn't know griffins made puns!"

"Most of us don't. I'm an unusual griffin." He shook his head and added, "In many ways."

Just then I heard Bibi calling. She sounded like she was right downstairs.

"That's my grandmother," I said. "I gotta go, otherwise she might come up here looking for me!"

"Go!" urged the griffin. "I can't afford to be seen by yet another human! But come back soon. *Please?*"

He sounded so lonely I couldn't help myself.

"I will," I said. "I promise!"

But I couldn't right away, because of who was waiting in the barn with Bibi.

That's all I can write for now. I'm being called for dinner.

Oh! Dinner makes me think of one more quick thing. I'm pretty sure I don't have to worry about Gerald wanting to eat me. If he were simply after food, he would have had me call for Bibi to come up to the loft, rather than urging me to hurry down so she wouldn't see him. Then he could have had two meals without much trouble.

So that's cool. I was hoping to make a friend this summer. I just never imagined it would be a griffin!

After supper, I'm definitely going back out to the barn.

Wednesday, July 1 (late afternoon)

My gamble of talking to the human paid off! His name is Bradley, and he seems to be a pleasant boy. It's hard to say for sure . . . we had only chatted for a little while before his grandmother called him and he had to hurry away.

I hope he will come back soon. It was good to have some company. Only now that he is gone I feel lonelier and more miserable than ever.

Should I go look for Master Abelard? I can't do it in the daytime, of course. And I wouldn't know where to begin anyway. He is so small he could be anywhere. For all I know he fell through some hole in the barn floor.

No! My teacher is smart and tough and resourceful. I am sure he is all right.

But why has he not returned?

What will I do if he never comes back?

And what about my family? To my surprise, I am really missing them. A lot.

7/1 (evening)

Holy farm cooking, Bibi's meals are heaven on a plate!

As planned, Herb came over for dinner. I get the impression he will be with us most nights.

I can't decide whether it's cute or weird that my grandmother has a boyfriend.

The downside to having Bibi cook is that I have to help with cleanup, since there is no dishwasher. Well, there's no machine that washes dishes. There is a dishwasher. His name is Herb.

Tonight I was the designated dryer.

(Heh. That's a good one!)

The funny thing is, I don't mind having to dry the dishes, even though it takes a lot longer than it does to empty the dishwasher at home, which is something I hate.

Maybe it's because I empty the dishwasher alone, but when I am drying the dishes, whether it's with Bibi or Herb, we talk. Herb is usually very jokey, but tonight he was in a serious mood and told me the story of how he lost his hand. I admire the way he deals with that. It's astonishing to watch him do dishes. He washes them faster with one hand than I can manage with two!

Even though I was enjoying our conversation, I was dying to get back to the barn so I could tell Gerald what had happened this afternoon. Here it is: When I came down from the loft Bibi was standing at the barn door. Next to her was a guy in some kind of uniform.

"Brad, this is Sergeant McConnell," Bibi said. "He wants to ask you a few questions."

"About what?" I asked nervously.

The man smiled. "Just checking up on something." He was trying to sound casual, but I could tell he was serious. "The other night, radar over at Huntsline picked up a strange, low-flying object during that big storm. We tracked it for a while but finally lost it. We think it might have crashed somewhere around here. Your grandmother tells me you like to ramble around in the woods, so I was wondering if you had seen any sign of it—maybe even just some scraps of metal?"

"Are you telling me you're looking for a UFO?" I asked.

He scowled. "I'd rather not use that term. So, have you seen anything?"

I shook my head.

"Well, if either of you does run across something, please give me a call. Here's my card, ma'am."

As he was driving off the truth hit me. What they had picked up on their radar wasn't a UFO . . . it was Gerald!

I can't wait to tell him about this. I think it's hilarious!

Wednesday, July 1 (early evening)

I spent the afternoon alternating between worry about Master Abelard and fear over what penalty I might face for having been seen by a human.

Despite that fear, I am desperately hoping the boy will come back. I need *someone* to talk to!

From the Notebook of Abelard Chronicus

◇◇◇◇◇◇◇◇◇◇◇◇◇◇◇◇◇◇◇◇◇◇◇

July 1 (later)

In the space of but a few moments I have experienced the best of all possible news and the worst of all possible news.

The best is simple and wonderful. After nearly three centuries, I have found my twin! Eduard is here in New Batavia, just as I had hoped he would be. It turns out he was away on a mission when that patrol found me, which is why they mistook me for him. I guess there was quite a fuss when he returned and they realized their error.

He showed up at my door about an hour ago, and we both burst into tears at finally seeing each other again. We jabbered away happily, thrilled at our reunion, until Magda, the woman in charge of my healing, insisted I had to rest. So Eduard bid me farewell and has returned to his family.

Alas, I cannot go with him, which is the bad side of the news. It turns out that if the gnomes who found me had realized I was not a citizen of New Batavia, they would have taken me to one of the humans who help keep the city a secret. No one is allowed entry here without permission . . . not even another gnome! It seems New Batavia is as strict about keeping its existence a secret as is the university and indeed all of the power structure of the Enchanted Realm. Clearly it was a mistake not to inform them I was not Eduard when I first awoke, as they now feel that I am untrustworthy. It makes no difference that I have a brother here and that I myself was a citizen of the original Batavia. They fear I might have turned on them and will reveal their location to the emperor. Once again my tendency to withhold the truth, to keep my secrets, has led me into trouble. Though in this case I don't know if telling the truth would have made any difference. The Batavians would still have held me under house arrest. It's particularly aggravating because I long with all my heart to explore the city.

Alas, they insist I must post bond before they will allow me out of this room, for fear I might make an escape attempt.

I have nothing to offer, of course, and I have only one way to get something . . . though the thought of asking for it almost sickens me with self-disgust.

Unfortunately, I see no other way.

Poor Gerald.

Wednesday, July 1 (late evening)

To my relief, Bradley reappeared an hour before it got dark. I was happy to see him, but he gave me some disturbing information when he said, "The reason I had to leave earlier was that someone was here looking for you."

Jumping up with a squawk, I cried, "Was it someone from the Enchanted Realm?"

I realized at once this was a silly question. No one from the Realm would have revealed himself to humans that way.

"Whoa, whoa, calm down!" said Bradley. "I didn't mean to frighten you."

"I wasn't frightened," I replied, trying to maintain a bit of dignity. "I was alarmed. It's different."

"Well, I didn't mean to alarm you. Actually, it's pretty funny. It was someone from the government. They picked you up on radar when you flew through the storm the other night."

"What is radar?"

Bradley thought for a minute, scowling as if it were hard to explain. Finally he said, "It's a way we have of tracking what's flying around."

"So it's a kind of magic!"

"No, it's not magic. It's science."

"Sounds like magic to me."

Bradley laughed. "According to my father—"

He stopped, and I could tell that for Bradley, as for me, the word "father" is packed with emotion.

"Go on," I said softly.

He nodded. "My father was a Grade A science fiction geek. He told me once that one of the greatest science fiction writers of all time, a guy named Arthur C. Clarke, had said that 'any sufficiently advanced technology is indistinguishable from magic.' So even though radar might sound like magic, there's a scientific explanation for it. Anyway, that's not the important thing. Here's why it was funny. They thought you were a UFO!"

I only understood about half of what he had just said. But rather than ask him about "science fiction" or what a geek is, I went for the most important question: "What is a UFO?"

"An unidentified flying object."

"But then they were right!"

"Of course they weren't."

"I was flying, right? And they didn't know what I was, right? Therefore, I was clearly an unidentified flying object."

Bradley sighed. "Well, yes. But when we talk about UFOs, we're really talking about ships from outer space."

"What is outer space?"

Bradley shook his head. "I'll explain some other time.

The important thing is you can relax. They have no idea you're here. They thought you were a . . . a flying machine and that you crashed somewhere in the woods. So there's no one looking for you, just for what they thought you were!"

I let out a sigh of relief. "You had me terrified," I said . . . then immediately wanted to bite off my tongue for admitting that I had been terrified.

"I'm sorry. I thought you would think it was funny."

"I do, now that you've explained it to me. Wait! Would this have anything to do with the green lights that shot past me when I was flying here?"

"Green lights? Holy Moses, dude. They were shooting lasers at you!"

"What are lasers?"

"More science . . . Just be glad they missed you!"

"I guess there's a lot we don't know about each other's worlds," I said.

Bradley agreed that this was true, so we talked about our worlds until it was almost dark.

It was very educational, especially the part about how most humans don't think things like griffins and dragons and unicorns are real.

I found this quite distressing.

When it was time for Bradley to return to the house, he said, "Is it all right if I come back tomorrow?"

"Please do," I replied.

It was a lovely conversation.
Here is today's poem.

All unexpected
I've made a new friend.
I'm glad we've connected,
But where will it end?

This is forbidden,
Another rule broken.
I should have stayed hidden.
I shouldn't have spoken!

I think I'm getting a little better! Have to stop now. The light is almost gone and it's getting too dark to write.

Wait! I have to put down one more thought. I just realized that I did not ask the most important question during my conversation with Bradley. When he talked about his father I should have asked, "Why did you say *was*?"

I feel bad that I was not thoughtful enough to realize that. Why do I always figure out what I should have done when the time for doing it is past?

Well, I can't think about that now. It is time to hunt. It will be easier to leave tonight, as Bradley showed me the loft door.

It's a strange door, because it opens onto nothing. A

human who stepped through would plunge to the ground, which is about twenty feet down.

"It's where the farmers used to bring in the hay and straw," Bradley explained as he demonstrated how to open it.

Flying out of this will be much easier than having to climb down that foolish ladder!

The moon is high, and it's time to hunt.

Watch out, bunnies, here comes Gerald!

I just wish they had the pink ones here. . . .

(Summer Assignment)

7/2 (Thurs.)

I like the Catskills. It is not as hot here as it is in the city. Also, unusual things can happen here.

One unusual place is my grandmother's barn. It is filled with old tools and machines. It is also a little bit scary, because it is so rickety that I am afraid it will collapse on my head.

My favorite thing is to go up to the lofts. They are mostly empty. Even so, you never know what you might find up there!

(3 paragraphs, 3 sentences each,
including 1 compound sentence.)

7/2

Holy freaking corned beef sandwiches . . . I've made friends with a griffin! A genuine, straight-out-of-myth, scary-big, weirdly gentle GRIFFIN!!!

I could hardly sleep last night thinking about it. This is not like last year. I am not sick, not delirious, not feverish. I am completely awake and alert. (I just pinched myself twice to make sure.)

Which makes me wonder if what happened last summer, the thing I had convinced myself was just a fever dream, might have been real after all.

So . . . about last year.

It was my first time visiting Bibi at the farm. Before that she had always come to visit us in the city. As near as I could tell, this had to do with Mom being stubborn about some old fight and refusing to go out to the country.

I love Mom, but she is a piece of work.

Anyway, whatever the reason, and to give Mom some credit, she decided that given the teasing I had been getting at school, what had happened with Dad, and the fact that I just wasn't all that "robust," it would be good for me to spend the summer in the Catskills with Bibi.

This was completely fine with me. I love Bibi and feel more safe and happy with her than with anyone else in the world.

Also, Dylan and Carter (my only two friends from

school) were going to be at camp, meaning I wouldn't have anyone to hang around with.

Problem was, it turned out my health was even worse than Mom had realized. Maybe there were some allergies involved; we're still not sure. Whatever the reason, by my third week here I was so sick I could scarcely get out of bed to pee.

Bibi was super-nice to me, but I could tell she was concerned. I was, too, when I was alert enough to think about it. A lot of the time I was in a haze, not sure whether I was dreaming or awake.

This had been going on for three or four days, and I could tell (when I was awake enough to tell anything) that Bibi was getting really worried. And then one night . . . I had to stop for a minute, because it feels so weird to be writing this down.

One night I was visited by gnomes.

At least that was what I *thought* happened. I truly had no idea if it was real or not. In fact, until now I figured it was a fever dream. But after yesterday I'm starting to wonder.

So it was the middle of the night . . . or maybe not. I was too groggy to tell. Let's just say it was dark outside my window. I was fairly zonked out but was roused by something moving on my pillow. I came more awake when I felt something touch the skin above my eyebrow. It was like Bibi's hand when she was checking my fever but not nearly as large—more like a fingertip than a palm.

I turned my head sideways and let out a yelp when I saw a tiny woman standing right next to my head!

She put her finger to her lips, signaling I should stay silent.

Given how loopy I was, it was easy enough for me to do so.

The woman was a little taller than my hand is long . . . five inches, maybe. This was added to by a tall, pointed hat. The bits of hair I could see beneath the edges of the hat were silvery white. She was built like a tiny version of Bibi.

While I watched, she climbed onto my chest and pressed her ear to my heart. When she stood again she scowled and shook her head.

That really scared me!

She walked back across me and down to the pillow. I turned my head to follow her progress and saw two more little people—obviously men, since they had thick white beards—standing on the bed.

The tiny woman climbed down to the men, and the three huddled together. They talked too quietly for me to hear, which was frustrating.

I struggled to stay awake but couldn't manage it.

The next thing I remember is being woken by the female making her way up my shoulder again. When she scrambled onto my face, I came to full wakefulness.

Or else that's when the fever dream kicked into high gear.

The woman pried at my mouth, which was very dry. When I opened it she took what looked like a tiny wine sack and pressed the spout between my lips. She squeezed the sack and something bitter squirted onto my tongue. I sputtered, but she held my lips together—she was remarkably strong—so I could not spit it out.

When I had swallowed the nasty liquid she climbed off my face. Once she was on the pillow she leaned close to my ear and whispered, "Be well!"

Then the three of them disappeared over the edge of the bed.

The next morning, I did indeed feel better . . . much better.

Bibi was delighted and clearly relieved.

And she asked me an odd question: "Did you have strange dreams last night?"

"Sure did," I said. "I dreamed I was getting medicine from little people!"

She smiled and said, "Ah, good."

I was still too woozy to think about what a weird response that was. And once the summer was over and I was back in New York, I figured the whole thing had just been a hallucination.

But now that I've met a griffin, I have to believe that anything is possible.

The Legend of Vande Velde's Landing

From *Myths and Magic of the Catskills*

By Trevor Montrose

One of the more unusual stories to be found in the Catskills is attached to a little town called Vande Velde's Landing, which is tucked away in one of the region's most rural areas.

The name of the town itself is a bit of an oddity. "Landing" would indicate a place where something came to dock. However, Vande Velde's Landing is located far from the mighty Hudson River and has only a medium-sized creek (or "kill," as the Dutch would term it) for waterfront—something that would hardly require a ferry for crossing.

So what is the reason for the name?

Gnomes!

At least that's what local lore would tell us. According to the legend, hundreds of years ago a migrating colony of Dutch gnomes made its way up the Hudson River, then by connected creeks westward to this isolated spot! This little town is where they pulled up their ships and decided to settle.

It is delicious to imagine a gnome ship, or perhaps several, each scarcely ten feet long, sailing the tributaries of the Hudson to this place. As gnomes are said to be but six inches tall, a ten-foot ship for them would be equal to a human three-master longer than 120 feet. For these little folk, such a vessel would have been half again as roomy as Henry Hudson's *Half Moon,* the ship that first navigated this river!

Lovely as the story is, it's hard to imagine how such a tiny ship, or ships, could have crossed the often tempestuous Atlantic Ocean. So how could the gnomes have reached these shores to begin with?

Whatever the reason, it's a matter of public record that in 1732 the name of the town was changed from Vande Velde's Corner to Vande Velde's Landing.

Surely something must have prompted this change of name!

To this day the townspeople are split into two elements.

One group, the Gnomists, celebrates the legend and claims to believe in the gnomes. Supporters of this approach tend to display statues of the familiar garden gnomes in their yards.

(Though this writer is sympathetic to the Gnomists' cause, I must admit their fervor sometimes goes to excess. I have personally seen front yards crammed with hundreds of the little statues and can state with certainty that it is a sight both alarming and tacky.)

The other faction is sometimes called the Deniers. However, this is not entirely accurate, as they do not deny the legend. Rather, they are resolutely silent about it. Among these folk, questions regarding the idea of gnomes having settled in the area are greeted with silence or, on occasion, outright hostility.

Few people, it would seem, are in the middle on the matter.

Consider this just one more charming quirk of the end-lessly charming and quirky Hudson Valley!

Thursday, July 2

Where, oh where, can Master Abelard be? His absence is driving me mad with worry!

It makes me restless to be trapped here in the barn all day. But I dare not go out until after dark.

I fear I would lose my mind if not for Bradley.

Here is today's poem.

I just made a friend named Bradley.
The truth is I needed him badly.
I'm alone and I'm frightened,
But my new friend has brightened
These days when I'm feeling so sadly.

Drat. I'm not sure the grammar is right on that last word. I should mention that Bradley has told me I can call him "Brad." Apparently this is something known as a nickname. From what I can make out, it is a sign of friendship and affection among humans.

Not wanting to seem unfriendly, I told him he could call me "Ger."

Hmmm. It looks funny when it is written that way. Maybe it should be "Jer." Or "Jare." Which looks weird but sounds right.

That I can consider this at all is due to the fine teaching of Master Abelard.

Master Abelard . . .

Sigh.

I should back up.

First off, Brad didn't come out to the barn today until fairly late in the afternoon. Naturally, this added to my nervousness and worries.

"Sorry I couldn't get here earlier," he said when he had climbed to the loft. "I had to go to town to help Bibi with some errands and it took longer than we expected."

At once I felt suspicious. Had the two of them gone to town to tell someone I am here?

I tried to beat down my fears. After all, you can't be friends with someone if you are afraid of them. The thing is, I have been told from before I could even fly that it would be disastrous to meet a human. Pushing past those years of warnings is hard.

After we had talked for a while I grew calm again. When Brad asked what had prompted me to leave the Enchanted Realm, I decided to tell him the story of my Hatchday(s). It seemed safe to tell the story here, since he couldn't tell it to anyone in the Enchanted Realm. Even more important, despite my occasional bouts of fretting, something in me really feels that I can trust him. And it felt good to get it out, to unburden my heart.

"Wait," Brad said shortly after I had started. "Do you mind if I record this?"

"What do you mean?" I asked.

He took from his pocket a slim black box. "This is a cell phone," he said. "I can do a lot of things with it. I'll show you. Hold still, and I'll take your picture."

He pointed the little box at me. I heard a clicking sound. Then he turned it around and said, "See! It's you!"

"How did you do that?" I squawked. Then I sighed and said, "I know . . . any sufficiently advanced technology . . ."

"You got it," said Brad. "Is it all right if I keep the picture? I can erase it if you want me to."

"It's all right," I said, flattered that he wanted to keep it.

"Now let me show you how I can record your story." He started tapping the little box, then said, "Okay, say something."

"Something," I replied.

"Very funny," said Brad. "Give me more to work with."

I started to tell him about my Hatchday, but I had only got out a sentence or two before he said, "Okay, that's enough. Now listen!"

He brought the box over to me, tapped it again, and played my own words back to me.

It was weird, and a little scary, to hear my voice coming out of that small box!

"Do I really sound like that?" I asked.

"Pretty much. It would sound better if I had big speakers, but yeah, that's your voice."

I wasn't sure I liked the idea of having my story recorded. But Brad said he thought it was important to get the experience down in my own words.

That might have been just flattery, now that I think of it, but it got me to agree.

7/2

This afternoon Gerald told me the story of his Hatchday.

I am not sure if it is fair to write it down. I know he would never do it himself, since it embarrasses him so much. On the other hand, I am trying to gather as much information as I can about griffins. I'm thinking about putting it all in a book . . . though I probably wouldn't try to publish it, since it needs to stay secret. Maybe I could turn it into a novel, the kind Dad and I liked trying to write together. I could even dedicate it to Dad.

Even if I never tackle such a book, I think it's good to keep an accurate record of this. Griffins, at least some of them, are clearly more sensitive than we would think.

So . . . here are Gerald's words, exactly as recorded on my cell phone:

✦   ✦   ✦

When my parents decided it was time to start a family, my mother laid three eggs, as griffin mothers normally do. The process is to lay one egg a day until the set is complete. The eggs do not start to develop until the third one is laid and the mother begins to brood upon the nest. Though maturation begins at the same time for all three eggs, and they should all hatch on the same day, it is expected that first laid will also be first hatched.

In this egg triplex, I was the one in that first egg. Had

I only been a bit bolder I would have been first hatched as well.

Oh, this is embarrassing!

✦ ✦ ✦

I cut out a brief section here that is nothing but my trying to convince Gerald to keep going. Finally he agreed.

✦ ✦ ✦

You must understand that when I began to stir in my egg I did not know where I was, or who I was, or even what I was. I knew only that I was cramped and should come out.

Using my talons—though I did not yet know that was what they are called—I poked a hole in the greenish wall that surrounded me. I now had an opening I could look through. What I saw beyond my wall was fascinating but also terrifying! I tipped myself back and forth so I could see more . . . and the more I saw the more frightened I became.

Outside was so *big*!

I did not know then, of course, that all I was seeing was my parents' cave, and that the real world was much, much bigger still!

Anyway, though part of me sensed I should break through the green wall, fear held me back and I decided to wait for a while before going further.

Even in the egg I was dithering!

In time, I slept.

When I woke—it was an hour later, as I eventually learned from my mother—I watched through my peephole as my sister gleefully burst out of her egg. I did not know that she was my sister or that her name was Violet. I only knew that someone else had broken a wall and come out and that I should do the same.

But I was still afraid.

Besides, the newly emerged thing was wet, her fur slick and her feathers bedraggled. It was not a pretty sight, and I didn't want to look that way myself.

I decided to continue waiting.

Not long after this my brother, Cyril, broke out of his egg. He appeared much as Violet had—though by this time she had dried out and was looking somewhat better.

Again, I wondered if I should also break down the wall and come out. Again I fell asleep instead, my brain baffled and befuddled by the choices facing me. What finally woke me—the next day, as I later learned—was my mother's voice. She had stepped up to my egg and, using what I can only call her Voice That Must Be Obeyed, she ordered, "Gerald Overflight, you come out of that egg right this minute!"

I was still frightened of coming out. However, I was even more frightened by my mother's voice! Reacting violently, I pecked my way out of the egg and tumbled onto the floor of my parents' cave.

My brother and sister looked at me as if they could not understand what I was . . . a look they have been giving me ever since. My father, who was perched nearby, put his right talons to his beak, pinched it, shook his head, and sighed.

I was only moments out of the egg and already I could tell that I had screwed up badly.

✦   ✦   ✦

That was where Gerald ended his story. As we talked about it, he explained that at the time his siblings were too young to understand the humiliation of being "first laid but last hatched" . . . and also too young to remember what had happened.

Unfortunately, a few weeks ago his mother told them the story. She did it with good intention, hoping to get them to understand that Gerald was somewhat timid by nature and that they should stop teasing him.

The result, of course, was the opposite. With this ammunition, Gerald's brother and sister began to humiliate him daily, making sure only to do so where their mother couldn't hear.

I understood this. I know all too well the secret ways of bullies. They hide themselves brilliantly. I totally get why Gerald felt it was necessary to run away from home.

Friday, July 3

I have good news and bad news. The good news is that there is word from Master Abelard!

The bad news is that what I have learned is horribly distressing.

The message arrived this afternoon while Brad and I were having a chat. We like telling each other about our worlds, and I was finding that doing so helped distract me from my worries.

I was telling Brad about the Encyclopedia Enchantica when we saw a rat crawl up from between two of the floorboards.

According to Brad, a rat in a barn is not that startling. He says what made this rat unusual was the roll of paper tied to its back.

Even more unusual was that it scampered directly toward me. (Any sensible rat would have fled in terror from my mighty talons and deadly beak!)

When it was about five feet away, it stopped, rose on its hind legs, and saluted.

I did the only thing that seemed to make sense: I lifted my right talons and returned the salute. I heard a click and knew that Brad had taken a photo of the moment.

The rat twisted around, pulled the scroll from its back,

and placed it on the floor in front of me. Then it turned, scampered away, and disappeared through the same floorboards.

"I am hopeful this may be from Master Abelard," I said to Bradley. "But will it be good news, or ill?"

"Well, why not open it and find out?" he replied.

When I didn't answer, he said, "Would you like me to do it for you?"

"Yes," I whispered, pushing the paper toward him.

Clearly he is a sensitive boy and understood my nervousness.

Brad reached forward and plucked the scroll from the floor.

I watched impatiently as he unrolled it. When he was done I said, "Well, what does it say?"

"Shall I just read it out loud?" he asked.

I thought about it for a moment, then nodded and braced myself for whatever the message might contain.

It was worse than I expected.

July 3

Dear Gerald—

I am sorry not to have been in touch with you. I suffered a serious accident two nights ago and was unconscious for quite some time. I hope you have managed on your own. I apologize for any distress I have caused you.

Since the accident things have gotten complicated, and far more difficult than I anticipated when you and I began this journey. To go straight to the point, I am being held in custody by the very people I was seeking when we came here!

My dear student, the following is hard for me to write. Trust that I am truly fond of you—really, you are one of the most gifted youngsters it has been my pleasure to work with. Even so, I must now confess that I have deceived and used you.

Specifically, I used you to carry me through the Transcendental Curtain . . . not for your own well-being but because I was desperate to reach the human world myself.

Why I needed to get here is a long story and not one I want to discuss right now.

In my own defense, I do think it was important for you to make this journey. I hope that in doing so you have gained the true treasure of confidence and independence.

(Alas, it may be hard to convince the Grand Council to count that as your Tenth Hatchday acquisition.)

Anyway, though I had personal reasons for joining you on this journey, I pray you will believe it was not my intent to abandon you after our arrival.

Unfortunately, things have not turned out as I had anticipated.

Not at all as I had anticipated.

I must now ask two things of you.

First: When the moon is at its highest point tonight, please come to the boulder that stands about three hundred yards behind the barn where you are (I hope!) safely sheltering. You will know the rock—it is just at the edge of the forest and is at least as tall as you are. If I cannot come myself, you will be met there by others on my behalf.

Second: When you come, please bring your bag of treasures.

Gerald, I am not nearly as good as you think I am. Even so, I hope you will believe that I did plan to remain with you to advise and guide you.

It is a great embarrassment that I now must ask you to rescue me instead.

You are a better student than I deserve.

Your teacher,

Abelard Chronicus

7/3

Sweet sizzling sausages, I never thought I would see a rat salute a griffin! I was glad I had my phone with me, because that was definitely a photo op!

When Gerald said the message was likely from his teacher, I wondered why it was so small. Then I realized (duh!) that it had to be small so the rat could carry it.

I did wonder how a griffin could have written something on such a tiny piece of paper. But who knows what kind of magic they have at their command?

I felt honored that Gerald allowed me to read him the message. (I offered because I could tell he was too nervous to read it himself.)

When I was done, Gerald and I sat in silence for a while. Finally I said, "Are you going to do as your teacher asks?"

Gerald hesitated for only a moment before saying, "I think I must." He ducked his head and cocked it sideways, which made him look oddly like a giant-sized version of the parakeet I used to have, and said, "Will you come with me?"

I had half hoped, half feared he would ask this. Going out in the middle of the night to help a griffin meet his teacher was about as cool a thing as I could imagine. But I also felt as if the world was stretching out in ways that my mind could barely contain.

Would this be dangerous? I didn't know.

What I *did* know was that if I turned down his invitation and didn't go, I would regret it for the rest of my life.

I thought about a poem called "Ragged John" we read in English class last year. I liked it well enough that I memorized it, though I never told anyone I had done that.

The closing lines are:

If a unicorn should call to you
Some moon-mad night, all washed in dew,
Then here's the prayer to whisper:
Grant me the heart to follow.

Gerald was no unicorn, but he was close enough for government work, as Bibi likes to say. And I might never again have such an invitation.

Seriously, who has ever had such an invitation?!

"Sure," I said. "I'll come with you."

The look on Gerald's face—really, he is amazingly expressive for someone with the head of an eagle—made me glad I had agreed to join him.

At the same time, it made me wonder what we would find when we got to the boulder. Who is holding Gerald's teacher captive?

It has to be someone or something very powerful.

After all, a griffin is a very powerful creature itself. And I assume this adult griffin doesn't have Gerald's dithering problem.

Maybe offering to go with him wasn't such a good idea after all!

I wonder if it's too late to back out.

Sheesh! Now I'm dithering, too!

No.

I've said I would go, and honor demands that I must!

Friday, July 3 (late evening)

I only have a little while to make these notes before it will be too dark to write.

Brad has returned to the farmhouse. His grandmother always expects him to come in when night falls. But he has promised to return when the moon is near its peak.

Will he? I hope so.

I have decided I like Brad. He seems to be about my age, in human terms, and everything I have sensed while talking to him makes me think he is someone I could be friends with.

Plus he likes puns! How lucky am I to find someone like that?

Friends with a human! My parents and the sibs would be appalled by the idea. But Brad is funny and kind and thoughtful, and I can tell he also wants to be brave and daring. What more could I ask for in a companion?

Alas, with Bradley gone, I have nothing to do but wait and wonder and fret.

Why couldn't Master A have confided in me about his real plans and asked me if I wanted to be part of his big adventure? I have admired him so much for so long, it is terrible to think that he had shut me out like this.

Yet he is still my teacher, and I owe him much. So I feel that I have no choice but to follow his request.

What will we find when we go to this boulder?

And why am I supposed to bring my treasures? They are sacred, and I must guard them with my life! Otherwise I am no true griffin!

Will I be asked to trade them for his freedom?

Could I do that?

Should I?

I think I would have to. But if I give up even one of the treasures, I don't think I can ever—EVER!—go home again.

Of course, I am not sure if I do want to go home again anyway.

Stop dithering, Gerald! Brace yourself for what is to come!

This is called "self-talk." It is a way of trying to convince yourself you can do something.

According to Master A it can be very effective.

I am not entirely convinced this is true.

From the Notebook of Abelard Chronicus

◇◇◇◇◇◇◇◇◇◇◇◇◇◇◇◇

July 3

Writing that letter to Gerald was one of the most humiliating things I have done in a long life that has seen more than its share of humiliations. (I do, after all, work in academia. . . .)

As I contemplate what I have dragged the griffling into, I grow ever more remorseful and ever more aware of how fond I am of him, despite his overly dramatic nature.

At the moment, I am feeling overly dramatic myself. That is because I had a visit this evening from my twin. The joy of finding Eduard again after almost three hundred years is nearly indescribable. I shall ever regret that I was off on my Wander Year when the gnomes of Batavia decided on their sudden escape to the New World.

"I was so torn!" Eduard told me tonight when we discussed this. "I wanted to stay with the city as we made our migration, but I was distraught that you were afield and nowhere to be found. And Mother was frantic, despite the fact that she was one of the prime movers of the migration. I tried sending messages—"

"I got them," I told him. "As soon as the first one reached me I hurried back to Batavia. Alas, I was too late.

By the time I reached the city it was already deserted. I cannot tell you how heavy my heart felt as I wandered those empty streets and recalled the words of your message. They are burned into my memory: 'Brother! We are going to a place where we cannot be found. I cannot tell you where it is, for we ourselves do not yet know. Hurry back to my side or I fear we shall be parted forever!'"

Tears stood out in Eduard's eyes. "I should have stayed," he murmured.

"If you had, then Mother and Father would have been without both of us for the rest of their lives," I replied. "No, you made the right choice."

After that our conversation moved to another matter, even darker than our separation.

It turns out that, true to our twinhood, Eduard and I have this in common: We pursue unpopular topics and bring distress with our research.

Only, what he has discovered exceeds in importance anything that I have worked on.

New Batavia is in imminent danger of destruction. Unfortunately, no one will believe him when he tries to explain the danger!

Friday, July 3 (night)

The moon nears its high point (which is how I have enough light to write this).

Where is Bradley???

7/4

Holy flying Butterball turkeys, have I got a lot to write about! I'm glad I carry this pocket journal . . . otherwise I wouldn't have anything to do that writing in, given where I am right now.

Hmmm. Better back up some.

Begin with this: I love being outdoors at night.

More specifically, I love being outdoors at night in the Catskills. I love the black velvety darkness, marked with points of light from the fireflies. I love the wet smell of the earth and the plants. Most of all I love the sense of magic in the air.

So I was excited (if also a bit terrified) to be going out to the boulder with Gerald last night.

As it turned out, he was even more on edge than I was.

In fact, he was a dithering mess.

I was amazed that someone as mighty as a griffin could be in such a state of fuss. I almost called him out for it but managed to stop myself before I said anything too insulting or stupid.

This morning Gerald and I spent some time comparing journals (well, he has a diary, I have a journal) because we're sharing a room right now.

I'm not going to repeat what he has been writing.

We've agreed we can combine our work if we ever want to make a book out of what happened to us.

(How cool is that? I have a griffin for a writing partner! I wonder what Dad would have thought of that. I so wish he could have met Gerald. I think he would have liked him.)

For now I'll just say that I wasn't expecting what we found when we went out to the boulder last night.

Even less was I expecting what happened next.

I'm torn between delight and horror.

Saturday, July 4

When I left off, I was in the barn, waiting for Brad, wondering if he would really show up.

I should have saved myself the fuss . . . a thing that is often true in my life. I had opened the loft door and was staring out at the night when a voice behind me called, "Hey, Gerald!"

I turned and was astonished to see not Bradley but a ray of light.

"What is that?" I yelped.

"It's just a flashlight," came Brad's voice.

"What is a flashlight? And if it is supposed to be flashing, why is it not going on and off instead of glowing in a steady beam? What kind of magic is this?"

"It's not magic at all."

"You have light coming out of your hand, and it's not magic?"

Brad laughed. "Not magic, just science. A couple of batteries and a lightbulb."

He might as well have said, "A couple of burblesnorts and a jiggle splat." However, I did not want to have this conversation again, so I simply said, "Thank you for coming. I wasn't sure you would."

Immediately I felt shame for admitting that I had doubted him.

"So, are we going out to try to find your teacher?" Bradley asked, ignoring my rude statement.

"Oh yes!" I cried. "Yes. I am ready to go. But could you help me with this?" I held up the pack that contained my treasures (and my diary, which is why I am able to write this now). "It is not easy for me to strap it on by myself."

Strapping it on was not easy for Brad, either, partly because he had to hold his "flashlight" in one hand (or sometimes his mouth) to see what he was doing.

"Jeez, I'm glad Bibi's friend Herb taught me how to saddle a pony last year," he said at one point.

"I am NOT a pony!" I replied sharply.

"Don't be so touchy. You may not be a pony, but you're as big as one. And Herb could do this with only one hand. But . . . oh wait! I think I've got it."

Unfortunately, this was not true. It took three more tries, as well as a lot of cussing from both of us, to get the pack in place. (The cussing turned out to be fun, but I won't write any of it down, as that kind of language is not very dignified.)

When we were finally ready I gestured to the loft door and said, "I'm going out that way. It will be easier than using that stupid ladder."

"Makes sense," replied Brad. "I'll go down and meet you behind the barn."

I leaped through the window and with only a couple of wing strokes glided to the ground. I landed gracefully, if I do say so myself.

Moments later Brad joined me.

"Ready?" he asked, and I could hear the tension in his voice.

"As I'll ever be," I replied, trying to keep the quiver and the quaver out of my own tones.

"The boulder that your teacher wrote about is back that way," said Brad, waving his arm. "I've climbed it many times."

"Then lead the way."

The night was surprisingly cool. A heavy dew had fallen, and soon the fur on my back legs was soaked. (My talons and the eagle portion of my front legs are waterproof, of course.) I considered flying, but I wanted to stay with Brad. Also, I didn't want to set off that "radar" thing he had told me about.

As we neared the boulder Brad whispered, "Looks like no one showed."

"Why do you say that?" I asked.

"If there was a griffin by the rock, we would see it by now."

"Why should there be a griffin by the rock?"

"Isn't your teacher a griffin?"

"What makes you think Master Abelard is a griffin?"

"Well, you're a griffin. So I figured your teacher must be a griffin, too."

"That is so human of you!"

"How do you know what's human?" Brad responded quickly.

He sounded angry, and I realized I had been careless. Master A taught me long ago that humans are very sensitive when it comes to having their assumptions challenged. It is better to lead them to the truth slowly. If pulled along too fast they seem to prefer to cling to their illusions.

"Sorry," I said. "That was rude of me. But why did you assume my teacher would be a griffin? Do you think all teachers and students must be of the same species?"

"Um . . . I guess not." Then he laughed and said, "In fact, I've had a couple of teachers that I'm pretty sure weren't human!"

I felt relief that the uncomfortable moment had passed.

"So what kind of, um . . . creature—"

"We prefer 'being,'" I said, interrupting.

"What kind of *being* is your teacher?"

"He's a gnome."

Bradley let out a cry of triumph. "Hah! I guessed there might be gnomes involved in this."

"Why in the world did you think that?"

"I'll tell you later. We're almost there."

He was correct. By the beam of Brad's nonflashing

"flashlight" I could see that we were close to the big rock. While there was no one in front of it, as we moved slowly around it we came to a group of gnomes.

Several of them cried out in alarm when they saw us.

"I warned you that he was a griffin," said Master Abelard, who was in the center of the group. (Well, I *thought* it was Master A.)

One of the other gnomes snapped, "Yes, we knew we would encounter a griffin. But you didn't say he would have a human with him!"

His insolence enraged me. "Shall I eat them?" I asked the gnome I thought was Master Abelard.

"Control, Gerald. Control," he replied, using the words Master A had repeated so many times when he was teaching me the finer points of being civilized.

Though it went against everything in my instincts, I stopped and took several deep breaths . . . which was lucky for the gnomes. After all, they were smaller than bunnies and would have been that much easier to swallow!

The one who appeared to be in charge stepped forward and said, "What is your connection to this human?"

"He is my friend," I replied. "His name is Bradley, and he came with me to meet my teacher, who is right there in your midst."

"Um . . . actually, that would be my brother," said the gnome I had *thought* was Master Abelard.

I let out a squawk. Brad put a comforting hand on my

neck, and I was happier than ever that I had asked him to accompany me.

"What are you saying?" I asked the gnome, who in every way possible appeared to be my teacher. "If you are not Master Abelard, then who are you?"

"I am his twin brother, Eduard. In a way, I am the reason you're here, since it was me who Abelard was seeking when he convinced you to come to the human world."

I felt dizzy.

"The problem is," Eduard continued, "my twin did not know that New Batavia is sealed against intrusion. As a result, he must undergo a trial for having entered the city uninvited." He paused, then added, "That's why we asked you to bring your bag of treasures."

My stomach knotted, and my heart began to beat faster.

My treasures!

Brad spoke up, earning my undying gratitude. "If Gerald has to ransom Master Abelard, it sounds to me like he was kidnapped, not arrested."

The head gnome had been staring at Brad. Suddenly he asked, "Are you from the Riddlehoover farm?"

"Yes. I'm visiting my grandmother for the summer."

One of the other gnomes stepped forward and whispered in the head gnome's ear. He nodded, then turned back to Brad and said, "Theo tells me we sent a healing mission to you last summer. Well, that's all right, then.

You are on the Temporarily Approved list. If you weren't, we would have to do something drastic."

"Approved for what?" asked Brad. "And what kind of drastic?"

"Approved to potentially be aware of us. We live in secret, and staying secret is necessary for our survival."

I noticed that he did not answer Brad's second question. But Brad replied with a third question.

"How secret can you be when there's a whole big story about the town having gnomes?" Brad asked.

The gnome smiled. "As long as most people think the story is a fun bit of folklore, it's useful to us, as it encourages others to *not* believe anyone who accidentally stumbles on the truth. These days a 'gnome-spotting' is almost always treated as someone trying to pull a prank. Even so, we must enforce strict rules about who can enter or exit New Batavia. Discovery by the human world would be a catastrophe."

I spoke up then, saying, "Master Abelard is a gnome, not a human. So why was it wrong for him to enter?"

"For reasons that range from safety to ancient grudge, we Batavians prefer to remain secluded from the Enchanted Realm as well as the human world. And to go back to *your* question, young human," he said, turning to Brad, "we are not asking for a 'ransom' for Abelard Chronicus. The treasures of Gerald Overflight are meant to serve as bond, to make sure Abelard does not flee before his trial."

"Does that mean I'll get them back after the trial is over?" I asked, feeling an enormous sense of relief.

"As long as your teacher makes his appearance in court, of course. Now, since you are here, we need both of you to come with us so we can assess whether you are a danger."

"Come with you where?" Brad asked.

"You'll see. You will be our guests for a few days."

"I can't be gone for a few days!" Brad cried. "My grandmother will be worried sick if I'm not home in the morning."

"We'll deal with that," the gnome replied. "Now, follow me."

7/4 (continued)

When the gnomes said they wanted us to follow them I figured we were going to some secret place where they wanted to . . . well, work out whatever it was they had in mind. I did consider bolting and running in the other direction, but since they had helped me get better last summer, I decided to go along.

Besides, for all I knew they had some kind of gnome magic that could stop me, or had set up some crafty gnome traps.

As we walked, the gnome who was in charge of the group said, "My name is Karel Hummel. You may call me Karel."

Something about him introducing himself that way made me feel a little more comfortable with him.

Then he said, "I will be in charge of your well-being while you are in our world." Which made me wonder if he was going to take us into the Enchanted Realm. I liked that idea, but I wasn't sure Gerald would be happy with it.

We started out, half the gnomes walking in front of us, the other half walking behind. It was slow going, for two reasons. First, the gnomes were so small—though I have to admit they moved pretty fast for people whose legs are only about three inches long. Second, it was not always easy for Gerald to follow them, since he had to keep tucking his wings against his sides to get between trees that were too close together for him to pass easily.

At last we came to what I knew to be the biggest tree in the forest behind Bibi's house, one I had seen many times on my rambles last summer. I couldn't put my arms even halfway around it. Roots thicker than my legs rippled out from it in all directions.

When the entire group had come to a stop, Karel slapped his hand against the thickest of the roots and shouted a word I didn't understand.

To my astonishment, a section of bark lifted up like a huge flap. It had been covering a doorway about six feet high and three feet wide. The door was vast compared to the gnomes but a good size to accommodate Gerald and me.

"This is the main stairway to New Batavia," said Karel. "You two must enter by this route. The rest of us will meet you below in the city."

I saw that one of the gnomes had opened a small door located at ground level, just inside the space Karel had revealed.

"Go ahead," said Karel. "The rest of us can't enter until we're sure you've gone in. You'll feel some pressure, but don't worry. It won't hurt you."

I glanced at Gerald and got a definite sense that this would go more smoothly if I went first.

So I stepped through the door.

Karel had told the truth. The instant I entered the

opening I felt pressure over my entire body. It was kind of like when you are swimming and go deep underwater. It wasn't painful, but it was definitely uncomfortable. Startled despite Karel's warning, I tried to back out. I couldn't! I could only move forward . . . forward and down, as what opened before me was a spiral staircase leading into the earth.

Gerald must have heard my surprised shout, because he asked if I was okay.

"I think so," I answered. "It just feels strange."

"All right, I'm coming in after you."

I was about four steps down and turned back to look. Gerald was forced to tuck his wings tightly against his sides to step through the opening. As soon as he was in, his eyes bulged and he cried, "What is this strange feeling?"

Like me, he tried to back up. When he found that he couldn't, his eyes grew even wider and he cried, "Brad! Brad, I'm being squashed!"

"It's okay," I said, hoping I was telling the truth. "The gnomes warned us about this. Just follow me."

I continued down the winding stairs. Looking ahead, the passageway seemed to be getting smaller, but not so small that I couldn't fit through it.

Behind me Gerald was muttering nervously. But he was sticking with me.

The stairway wound down . . . and down . . . and down . . . and DOWN!

The pressure grew ever stronger. It was like diving

into a lake, then going so deep you think your ears are going to pop.

"Gerald, are you all right?" I called.

"I think so, Bradley. And we can't stop here. We must keep going."

I continued downward, fighting the discomfort. Every few steps I thought my head was going to bump against the roof of the stairwell.

It never did.

I should have realized what was happening. I think my mind was just refusing to accept it.

Finally I came off the last step, onto a small landing.

Ahead of me was a green door. I waited for Gerald, then opened it and stepped through.

Saturday, July 4 (continued)

The gnomes shrank us! When we came out at the bottom of that crazy stairway, Brad was *shorter* than a gnome (as he is still a boy). I was only a little bit taller than one myself.

"Welcome to New Batavia," said Karel.

"What have you done to us?" cried Brad . . . which was silly, as it was perfectly obvious what they had done.

"Merely arranged it so you could fit here," replied Karel. "Don't worry, it's not permanent."

"The shrinking won't wear off while we're down here, will it?" I asked as I had a sudden, horrifying vision of growing back to my normal size and being wedged into this miniature underground world, unable to move!

"Of course not! It can't. The only way to return to your regular size is to walk back up the stairway . . . which you will be allowed to do when the time is right."

"Does that mean we're prisoners?" Brad asked.

"We are asking that you not leave the city for now. But you will not be imprisoned in a cell or anything like that. Indeed, you will be free to roam about and study our world as much as you wish."

That sounded good. But then a stern look crossed Karel's face and he added, "At the end of your visit we will have a hearing to determine whether it is safe to let you return to the world above."

I did not like the sound of that, not at all!

7/4 (continued)

My first sense of the place we had come to was that it was enormous, almost impossibly big for an underground world.

Then I realized that it wasn't nearly as big as it seemed—it was just that I was so much smaller than I'm used to being!

I'd been hoping I would grow a few inches this year. This was like the ultimate ungrowth spurt!

It is totally freaky to think about . . . which might be why I keep seeing this place as if it's scaled to my normal size. My brain is refusing to accept that I'm only four and a half inches tall!

I was also extremely upset about Karel's threat that we might be kept here forever. I wonder what Bibi would have to say about that, since she seems to have a connection to the gnomes.

Setting aside my worries, I was fascinated by the place we had entered, which was a virtual underground city.

"There's a human town named Batavia," I said. "In New York State, over near Buffalo."

(Geography is one of my better subjects, though you wouldn't know it from my grades.)

"We had the name first," Karel replied. "We brought it with us from the old country."

"When did you come here?"

"Nearly three hundred years ago. Now come along . . . we'll show you to your rooms, and I'll leave you something you can read to get a little of our history."

New Batavia was dimly lit, reminding me of the twilight world described in Sherlock Holmes stories, when it is dark in London and the city is illuminated by gas lamps.

In fact, there were actual gas lamps all along the wide avenue we were now following. (No fog, though, so it was not quite Sherlockian.)

When I asked what powered the lamps, Karel answered, "A fuel we distill from the sap of pine trees. We created the process ourselves."

I could hear pride in his voice when he said this. Gnome technology!

The avenue had many curves and turns. This was because it had to wind around the tree roots that enter from the top of the world, then continue down through the "floor." Also it was lined with houses, each neat and trim. Some were made of wood, others of stone.

Gnome children played in many of the yards. Some were romping around with mice and chipmunks that were clearly their pets. I was dying to take a picture of that, but given the gnomes' desire for secrecy that would clearly have been a bad idea!

Children and adults alike stopped to stare as we went past. I figured this was partly because I was a human, but even more because Gerald is a griffin.

After a little while we came to a large (in gnome terms) stone building, half again as tall as all but the biggest of the houses.

A sign out front said TUCKER'S TAVERN.

"This is where you will lodge," said Karel. "It's a comfortable place, and the rooms are decent. Your meals will be provided in the tavern's main dining room."

Turning to Gerald, he said, "If you will hand over your treasures now, I will give you a receipt for them. Once we finish the paperwork your teacher will be free to join you here. As long as he does not flee before his hearing, the treasures will be returned to you when it is over."

Gerald looked at me, and the pain in his eyes almost made me cry out. I knew his treasures were important, but until that moment I had not understood how truly *vital* they were to him.

"Will you undo the pack, Brad?" he asked in a small voice.

I did as he asked and could feel him trembling as I worked the straps. I handed the pack to Karel, who passed it to one of the other gnomes and said, "Inventory the contents and write up a detailed receipt."

I heard Gerald stifle a sob as Karel led us into the tavern.

I like old buildings, and the inside of Tucker's Tavern, with its polished dark brown wood and its stone-paved floor, was beautiful. Rich smells from the kitchen made my mouth water, though I knew it would be a long time before breakfast.

If not for the fact that I was still kind of freaking out about being only four and a half inches tall, I would have been very happy to stay in this place.

Karel led us to our room. To my surprise, there was a bed for me . . . and a nest of some sort for Gerald.

Karel must have read the expression on my face, because he said, "We knew from Abelard that we would be welcoming a griffin, so we prepared this nest for him. We were not expecting a human youth as well, but it was easy enough to have a bed moved in here."

So we may be prisoners of a sort, but at least our captors are very thoughtful.

When the gnomes had left us, Gerald said, "I am so sorry, Brad. I had no idea when I invited you to join me tonight that this is how things would end up."

He sounded on the verge of tears. I couldn't tell if that was because he was frightened, because he felt guilty about having brought me into this situation, or because of his treasures. Maybe all of those things.

"It's all right, Gerald," I said, trying to sound braver than I felt. "I don't think they're going to hurt us. And as long as they let my grandmother know where I am—I have to trust them when they say that they will do that— then I'm kind of enjoying this. It's an adventure!"

"I wish I felt the same way," he said miserably. "But I'm too worried about my treasures."

Then he explained to me about griffins and treasures.

I was fascinated by all this. I also wanted to tell Gerald that Master Abelard sounded like a real jerk. But I figured that might not be the best thing to say right now.

Instead, I said, "Here's that book Karel said he was going to leave for us! Let's take a look."

THE REBELLION OF THE BATAVIAN GNOMES

From *The True History of the Lost City of Batavia*
(Limited edition, published by New Batavian Press)
By Joosten Van Meer, Gnome in Exile

In the early 3400s (or 1700s, as humans count the years) the rulers of the Enchanted Realm in Europe, and most especially the emperor (under whom all beings, from elf to gnome to griffin to dragon, serve), decided it was time to make the barriers between the human world and the Realm more rigid.

So it was that an edict went out that all of the Enchanted, even those who had close ties to the human world and had long made their homes there, were to return to the Enchanted Realm and shut themselves off completely from the human world.

The reason for this was sad but, most feel, inevitable. As the Age of Enlightenment dawned in Europe, the human world was becoming ever less welcoming to magic and enchantment.

With some grumbling, most of the Enchanted agreed to this division. Many were relieved. Others mourned to lose their connection to the humans.

One group, the gnomes of Batavia, a small underground city in Holland, rebelled entirely against what they considered this unnecessary isolation. The leaders of the city felt that a continued connection to the human world was vital for both worlds.

Most especially Sophentrina Chronicus, one of the city's designated Wise Women, argued this point. Though she was voted down in the emperor's court, her arguments were embraced by the Batavians themselves.

While some groups, such as the Enchanted Animals of the Deep English Forest, resisted the idea of separation well into the nineteenth (by human reckoning) century, the Batavian gnomes took a bolder route. They voted to undertake a mass migration to North America, where the strictures regarding separation of human and Enchanted were not yet so fierce, and the emperor's reach was limited.

Their journey was made possible in part by the aid of a group of renegade elves.

The preparations were magnificent to behold. In secret, and in return for the greater part of the Batavian treasury, the elven shipyard prepared two dozen beautifully crafted vessels, each large enough to hold two hundred gnomes.

The idea that the gnomes of Batavia disappeared overnight is a bit of an exaggeration. It actually took our people three nights to load all their household goods onto the ships. When all were on board, the little ships, far too small to sail on the sometimes storm-tossed waters of the Shadow

Sea, were picked up by large cranes and loaded onto three elven ships, which were to carry them to the distant shores of the American continent.

The sea journey was without incident. However, once the gnome ships were offloaded and passed through the Transcendental Curtain into the human world (something that was considerably easier to do at that time), the Batavians had adventures enough to fill a book as they made their way up the Hudson River and through various streams and rivers to the little town of Vande Velde, where they chose to settle, and which was eventually renamed Vande Velde's Landing in honor of this event.

The sudden abandonment of Old Batavia caused enormous distress in the highest ranks of the Enchanted Realm. The emperor's first response was unbridled fury. Many a courtier still carries a gem that shattered the day the emperor shouted his rage. They keep these as reminders of how terrible his wrath can be.

Once his anger had time to cool, it suited the emperor and the powers of the Faerie Court to send out conflicting stories about the vanishing of the Batavian gnomes, thereby sowing confusion about what had really happened. This, they felt, was better than letting it be known that the gnomes of Batavia had simply refused to bow to their authority. The emperor's greatest fear was that if this became known it would lead to further rebellion. So the choice was made to silence all word of what the Batavians had actually done.

Thus it is that from that day until the present, the continued existence of the Lost City of Batavia has remained a state secret in the Enchanted Realm. Indeed, to the best of our knowledge no one there has any idea where our city is now located.

A strict ban on research into the matter has long been in effect, and any scholar foolish enough to defy this censorship is subject to immediate dismissal and banishment.

Even to speak of our existence is forbidden.

Which is completely fine with the citizens of New Batavia!

Sunday, July 5

This morning Master Abelard rejoined us. He is staying in the room next to ours.

I was startled when he appeared at our door. It was not just that it felt strange to be only a bit taller than he is, rather than towering over him. What shocked me even more were the bandages and the crutches.

"What happened?" I cried. "Did the Batavians do this to you?"

"No, no," said Master A. "This is the result of an altercation with an owl. It's how I ended up here."

Then he told us the story of how he escaped the owl's clutches and was carried here unconscious. He also spoke at length about his remorse at having dragged me into this. By all appearances, he is stricken with grief and guilt over having endangered my treasures. Unfortunately, I am confused as to whether I can believe him in this regard, as I now understand him to be a master of deception!

I feel a poem coming on:

Abracadabra,
Magic and fire,
My teacher's a phony,
A big rotten liar!

Oh my. That one just sort of poured out. I'm not very proud of it. On the other wing, I have to say that it is true to the way my heart feels right now.

Brad has offered to write up a description of the underground world we now inhabit. I am too distraught to do this myself, so I have accepted his offer.

July 5
Report to the City Elders
from Eduard Chronicus

Revered colleagues,

Despite resistance from some of you, I have been out and about in the Up Above, and what I have to report is not good.

Though the matter is not completely settled, it seems increasingly likely that the human government is about to approve the areas beside our home as the best spot for the DeFelice Wetlands Preservation Project.

The project is being planned with good intent. Indeed, it will be very good for waterfowl.

Unfortunately, if it is put into action, the plan's effect on our city will be devastating.

In short, it will submerge New Batavia.

To be clear: If we do not take preparatory action, there is a serious chance that the city will be underwater before we know what is upon us!

Will we literally drown, as some of you have accused me of saying? Of course not. We will have warning, thanks to our friends in the Gnome Protective Association, and we will make our way out in time.

But the loss of goods and property will be overwhelming.

Worse, we will be stranded Up Above! I hardly need stress the dangers if *that* happens!

Our human friends are working as hard as they can to prevent this catastrophe. However, human politics have changed in recent decades, and individual voices are drowned out (just as our city shall be drowned) in the current climate.

Is it certain that this project will be approved?

No.

Are the chances are good that it will be?

Yes.

With that in mind, is it not folly for us to refuse to prepare for the possibility of disaster?

Respectfully submitted,

Eduard Chronicus

Citizen

7/5

Festering bags of sauerkraut! I just realized I've got a *big* problem. I was supposed to send off my journal entries yesterday! Mom is going to kill me if I am not allowed back into WIPS this fall!

I am also feeling awful for Gerald. I know he loves his teacher, but he's having a hard time forgiving Master A for what he's done. It's obvious that it was really bad, but I have a sense that I can't fully understand the depth of how hurt Gerald feels.

I think it must be some kind of a griffin thing.

Anyway, thanks to Gerald's treasures, Master Abelard has been set free. I met him for the first time this morning.

I am not sure how to feel about him. He is clearly smart and funny. In fact, he reminds me a bit of Herb. But I know too much about what he has done to easily trust him.

Well, enough about Gerald's teacher. Right now I want to describe the city. That's because Karel gave me a tour this morning, and I need to get my impressions down while they're fresh in my mind. (Also, I promised Gerald I would cover this.)

Oh! One other thing first. The gnomes brought me a message from Bibi. It was in her handwriting, so unless they are extremely tricky, that means they did indeed tell her where I am. She says she might join us here soon!

I knew my grandmother was an amazing person. As it turns out, I didn't know the half of it!

I wonder if Herb will be coming with her.

Anyway, back to New Batavia.

The first thing to deal with is the matter of size. I've spent a lot of time working on this, partly so I can get it clear in my own head, partly so I can try to explain it.

Start with this: The average height for an adult male gnome is six inches, which is half a foot (as measured by a ruler, not an actual human foot, since those can vary greatly). Since it takes two gnomes to equal a foot, a six-foot-tall human is twelve times taller than the average gnome.

Using twelve-to-one as my basis, I've been making some calculations. As near as I can make out, a medium-sized gnome house is about two feet wide and four feet long. (About 24 feet by 48 feet if it were human sized.)

Allowing for a lawn and garden, you could still fit well over a thousand gnomish houses onto a football field! So though New Batavia appears to stretch on for nearly a mile in all directions, it is not nearly as huge as it first seemed to my newly shrunken self.

Even so, it's pretty dang big. I mean, there's an entire city down here, spread over three levels of caves!

Yes, three levels! There are stairs and slides (so cool!) and even squirrel-powered elevators to take you from one level to another.

However, "caves" is not really the right term, as Karel made very clear.

More about that later.

I mentioned the houses before, but there are also schools and libraries (one of each on each level) and shops and taverns. Additional spaces are set aside as public areas, though you couldn't really call them parks, since there's no grass or trees. Well, there are tree roots. But it's not really the same thing. Lots of mushrooms, though, which are often waist-high or more for the gnomes. (Well, for me, too, at the moment.)

According to Karel, about six thousand gnomes live down here.

They built their underground world around the roots of the trees, and those roots are part of what keeps it stable. It makes for a strange look, though, since curved, knobbly wooden pillars stretch from the "sky" to the ground. There are lots of them, and often houses are tucked against them or even use a curved one as part of the roof.

I put "sky" in quotation marks because what's above us is not really sky, of course. The problem is "roof" and "ceiling" aren't the right words, either. And since the gnomes don't like to think of their underground world as a cave or cavern, I can't call it the cave-top.

"Caves are natural things," Karel explained as we were walking down a side street. "This world is one we made ourselves, carving it out from the earth, and we are proud of that!"

Anyway, since I have no other word for what covers us, I'll use the gnome word for it, which is "skroothaben."

The thing to know about the skroothaben is that it's not bare dirt. The entire surface is covered with a strong mesh that prevents "dirt rain." This mesh is woven by the women of the colony, and it has never failed, which is why the gnomes like to say that the women of New Batavia hold up the sky. (They should probably say "hold up the skroothaben." I guess they just think "sky" sounds better in that sentence.)

Embedded in the skroothaben are thousands of gently glowing disks.

When I asked Karel about them, he said, "I was happy to tell you about the streetlights. The skylamps, however, are not for discussion."

I found this answer annoying, but also pleasantly mysterious.

The streetlights and the skylamps go dim at certain hours, to create a kind of night, and grow brighter for "morning."

However, it is never truly bright down here.

"Do you ever go outside?" I asked Karel.

"Oh yes. We call it 'going Up Above.' We go out quite frequently. It is not good to spend all your life underground. We mostly venture out after dark, of course, or early in the morning, as there are less likely to be humans around at those times."

Then he explained that they have an enormous system of spy holes and mirrors set up, to keep an eye on the woods and help them be aware of intruders.

"We are also protected by some of the humans in town," added Karel. "There are many times we would have been in great danger without their assistance. In return we provide medical care for their families, something we are very good at, as you may remember."

"Boy, do I," I said. "I was never sure whether that was a dream or reality."

"Well, now you know the truth," Karel replied.

"So, the Gnome Protective Association is actually a real thing?" I asked.

"Of course it is," Karel replied. "Your grandmother is the president."

July 6

My Dear Colleagues,

We have heard the report from the alarmist Eduard Chronicus, and I wish to start my own remarks by noting that he is brother—twin, no less!—to the recent intruder Abelard Chronicus ... that same gnome who took advantage of us by not revealing his true identity when we had brought him to safety and nursed him to health. Instead, he let us believe that he was his brother and therefore belonged here.

Now let us consider that brother, Eduard. The standard view of Citizen Chronicus is that he is the sort who would set his hair on fire and run in circles at the sight of an aggressive cricket.

He is not, however, representative of the grit and reserve of this council, and this city.

To be brief, this fancied threat of his, of the drowning of New Batavia, is sheer nonsense. Our human protectors have always kept us safe from this sort of thing, and there is no reason for us to think they will fail us now.

To divert so many of our resources, and so much of our wealth, to preparing for an utterly unlikely catastrophe strikes me as the height of folly.

We have better things to do with our time and money!

Monday, July 6

Brad's grandmother and her boyfriend have joined us!
("Boyfriend" is a new term to me and seems odd for a man who is clearly on the edge of old age.)

Though we were glad to see them, they have come with terrifying news. It seems that some water project (I can't say too much about it—I don't understand these things) has been approved despite their best efforts to prevent it.

As a result, New Batavia is in danger of being put underwater!

Master Abelard is both subdued and jubilant. Subdued for many reasons, including the fact that this is terrible news. But also jubilant because it proves that what his twin brother has been trying to convince people of is true.

(How could I not have known that Master A has a twin?!)

Anyway, now that Eduard's news has been confirmed, the entire city is in a state of flustered dithering that makes *me* seem like the calmest creature who ever lived! Terror and cries of doom are everywhere!

Clearly, Bibi (she told me I could call her that) and her boyfriend are trusted voices, for no one has questioned their report.

This afternoon we held a meeting in our room.

In attendance were Brad's grandmother; her boyfriend, Herb; Master A and Master Eduard; Brad; myself; and Karel Hummel . . . whose first words on entering the room were "I'm not here!"

Which I took to mean that his attendance had to be a secret.

Shortly after we gathered there was a knock at the door and another human stepped in.

"Lukas!" cried Bibi happily.

"Lukas?" asked Brad. "As in Great-Uncle Lukas, the painter?"

"That would be me," said the man cheerfully as Bibi ran to hug him.

"But I thought you were dead," said Brad.

"I didn't tell you he was dead," Bibi said. "I told you he was gone. About thirty years ago he chose to live in New Batavia. Well, chose with some persuasion from the gnomes. They were afraid the pictures he was painting might give them away."

"I was getting a little careless," confessed the man. "I don't regret the choice, though. I've been very happy down here."

Karel Hummel cleared his throat and said, "As I should not be here at all, I cannot stay long."

"Then let's get down to business," Bibi replied. "My brother and I can catch up later."

Master Eduard (that seems the best term for him, since he is Master Abelard's twin) started by thanking Bibi and Herb for confirming what he had been trying to tell the city council.

"I wish we had not been forced to do so," said Bibi. "All of us in the Protective Association have tried so hard to avert this situation."

"Is there anything that could change the decision?" asked Brad.

"Not much," said Herb glumly. "The only thing that might make a difference is if we could prove there's an endangered species on the land. In that case they would be forced to go to the second-choice spot for the project."

"Wouldn't gnomes count as an endangered species?" Brad asked.

Herb chuckled, the three gnomes scowled, and Bibi said, "You might be able to make that case, except for the fact that the whole point is to let the Batavians remain secret. Besides, the term 'endangered species' definitely refers to plants and animals. Finding a genuine endangered species would take a minor miracle."

Suddenly Brad leaped to his feet and cried, "I think I'm about to come up with a miracle!" Turning to Bibi and Herb, he said, "How much time do we have?"

"A week, maybe two at the most," Herb replied. "The time for challenges to the decision has nearly expired. Things are moving fast now."

Brad nodded. "I have an idea. I don't know if it will work, but at least hear me out."

Everyone signaled that they were willing to listen.

"Okay, here it is: What if we could bring in a new species, one that had never been seen here before?"

"What are you talking about?" asked Herb.

Turning to me, Brad said, "Gerald, what is your favorite food?"

"Bunnies," I answered without hesitation.

"What kind of bunnies?"

"I like the pink ones best," I replied. "But I can't get them here."

"There you go!" Brad cried. "Pink bunnies! What if Gerald went back to the Enchanted Realm, caught some pink bunnies, and brought them here to release? They would certainly qualify as an endangered species. You'd only have to look at them to know they were the only ones ever seen in the human world!"

"I don't know, Bradley," Bibi said. "Introducing a new species can have terrible consequences. Look at the rabbit situation in Australia."

"But it's not the same, dear," put in Herb. "When rabbits were introduced into Australia, they were a totally foreign species and had no natural predators. We already have rabbits here, just not pink ones." Turning to me, he said, "Gerald, how different are your pink bunnies from the rabbits you've been catching since you got here?"

"Not much," I said. "They're a bit sweeter, is all. And maybe a little bigger."

"Doesn't sound that disruptive to me," said Brad's great-uncle Lukas.

"But how do we get them?" Eduard asked.

"I am a great bunny catcher!" I replied. "If I can get back to the Enchanted Realm I will happily gather some bunnies to bring back . . . even if it means I have to catch them without eating them!"

"But can you catch them without *hurting* them?" Bibi asked. "When eagles catch a rabbit, their talons dig right into it. There's no point in bringing back a bunch of dead rabbits."

This made me laugh. "Eagles are much smaller than griffins. Their feet are not big enough to hold a rabbit without digging into its sides. My mighty talons can easily wrap around a bunny!"

"This might actually work," said Herb. He stood and began to pace, as if he were too excited to sit still.

"I believe you're right," said Master Eduard.

"Even so, it will not be easy," said Master Abelard. "Gerald, your beak and talons are meant for rending and tearing, not capturing and caring. Plus your instincts are all for eating."

"I know," I moaned, thinking of the deliciousness of the bunnies.

"I think I can help!" said Brad. "If I go *with* Gerald I

could take the bunnies from his claws and put them in . . . um, whatever we need to bring them back in."

"Perhaps the women who hold up the sky could weave some nets for you!" cried Master Eduard.

"My wife is leader of one of the weaving groups," Karel said. "I believe she has a good amount of mesh on hand right now. She could make some carry sacks pretty quickly." He looked at me and said, "Probably it would be best to make a set of two, with a connection across the middle that would let Gerald sling them over his back."

"How many bunnies would we need?" Brad asked.

"The more the better," Herb answered. "Some to prove that we're not making this up, others to set free on Agatha's land so that the investigators we call in can find specimens on their own and verify their presence."

"Oh, wait," said Brad's great-uncle Lukas. "What's to keep the rabbits from leaving this area and going somewhere else? They won't do us any good if that happens."

"Don't worry about that," Karel said. "We have whole teams of rabbit-wranglers. We can keep them close by with no problem."

At Herb's words "the more the better," I had had a stupefying thought: What if I could get my horrible sibs to help with this? If all three of us came back here with bulging packs of bunnies, the effect could be overwhelming!

I saw two things that might help me to convince Violet and Cyril to join this mad project.

1) It would involve catching bunnies, which they like to do at least as much as I do. On the downside, we would have to forgo eating them, which they would not like. But they enjoy the hunt as much as the feast, so maybe that wouldn't be a problem.

2) I could challenge the sibs to come to the human world—a thought so daring it would make me seem unbelievably bold in their eyes.

Short version: I loved this idea!

"Have her make three sets of bags if she can," I said to Karel. "I am going to try to enlist some help!"

7/6

Holy magic meatballs, I'm going to the Enchanted Realm!

Of course, there were complications with my plan.

First of these was that Gerald and I would have to get big again to carry it out. Getting big was easily enough accomplished—all we had to do was go back up the shrink/grow stairway.

The problem was, we had to get permission to do that.

Which was why it was a good thing Karel Hummel was on our side and was convinced that what we were going to do was necessary.

"I can't get permission," he said. "But I can get you into the stairway anyway."

What he didn't say, but was very clear, was that he would be doing this at great personal risk.

Next Herb pointed out that I would need gloves to handle the rabbits. "'Bunnies' may sound fluffy and harmless," he said. "But they have claws and sharp teeth, and wild ones do *not* like being handled!"

"I left a pair of work gloves on the kitchen counter," Bibi said. "They're thick and sturdy, and should be about the right size for Brad."

Next was the issue of how we were to enter the Enchanted Realm. The best way would be for Master Abelard to guide us. But if he left the colony before his trial, Gerald's treasures would be forfeit! So that idea was out.

In the end, Master A simply explained to us that since Gerald belonged in the Realm, all we had to do was go three times widdershins around a church. Since there was a fairly isolated little church not far from Bibi's farm, that would not be a problem.

"What if someone is waiting to arrest me once I go back to the Realm?" asked Gerald.

"I wouldn't worry about that," said his teacher. "Unless someone has done some deep research, they won't be looking for you to come in where you will." (I knew it was Master Abelard speaking and not his brother because his boots were black, whereas Master Eduard's were a rusty brown. It was the only way I could tell them apart.)

Once all that was settled, Master A said he wanted to have a private conference with each of us, to give us a pep talk. There was some fuss about this, but finally the other adults agreed.

I went first.

"There's something you need to know about returning from the Enchanted Realm to the human world," he said when we were seated in his room.

Then he told me that according to the lore and rules of the Realm, Gerald would have to fly full-speed headfirst into a solid rock wall to come back to this side of the Transcendental Curtain.

"You've got to be kidding!" I cried.

He shook his head. "I am quite serious. And the common belief is that anyone trying to go through one of those walls must do so with absolute confidence, total assurance that the wall will yield. If not, it will remain solid and you will smash into it and die."

"I don't think I can manage that," I said, my voice weak.

Master Abelard smiled. "You don't have to."

"What do you mean? I have to come home!"

"I mean, it's not true. The idea was put out as a way to prevent excessive traffic between the two worlds. In truth, the wall yields whether you believe it's going to or not. Perhaps I should have told Gerald this, but I think it was good for him to believe in his belief, if you see what I mean. He needs more confidence, and his success in going through the cliff the first time was good for him."

"So why are you telling this to me?"

"Because Gerald will probably mention it to you, and I feared you might choose to remain in the Realm rather than risk death trying to return."

"Oh" was all I could say.

"It *will* be important to make sure you're flying toward the right cliff. Gerald *should* be able to recognize it, but he may have been so panicked the first time that he won't be sure. So I want to give you some landmarks."

Then he described a series of peaks and cliffs I should watch for to be sure we were on track. The landmarks sounded very clear. Even so, I wrote them down in my pocket journal. This was a world where I had never been, and now I had the task of making sure we flew through the *right* stone wall so that we wouldn't die in the process!

I was about to back out, but then I thought about Dad and how much I want to be worthy of him.

Excerpt from remarks at memorial service for Dr. Arthur Ashango

Dear Friends—

We have gathered today to celebrate the life of Arthur Ashango, a good man taken from us far too early.

Dr. Ashango—Art, as most of us called him—had a thriving practice here in New York City. However, he also was committed to doing volunteer work with Surgeons for Peace, making two trips a year to provide free medical services in underprivileged countries. A passionate advocate for children, Art did most of his work in connection with orphanages.

Sadly, during his last trip, his medical work was interrupted by a massive earthquake. Being who he was, Art immediately plunged into the orphanage connected to the clinic where he had been working. The condition of the building was perilous, and there were numerous children trapped within. That twenty-three of those children are alive today is due to his selfless courage. He pushed the twenty-third of those children ahead of him, propelling the little girl out of the building just before it collapsed.

I have known many good men in my life. Arthur Ashango was the best of them. I join with his wife, Delia, and his son, Bradley, in mourning his death. Despite their great loss, I hope Delia will forever cherish her husband's courage and humanity, and that Bradley will see in his father a model of the kind of man he may become himself.

Though he was taken too soon, his mark is indelible.

Dr. Paul Miller
Pediatric Surgeon
Danziger Memorial Hospital

Monday, July 6 (continued)

After Master Abelard's mysterious meeting with Bradley, he called me in. I crouched on the floor in front of him, still startled to be looking him in the eye instead of gazing down at him!

To my surprise, he held in his hand the armband from Alexander the Great.

Looking at me solemnly, he said, "At great personal risk, Karel Hummel removed this from the courthouse in order that you might wear it on your journey to the Enchanted Realm."

"Why bother?" I said, a trifle bitterly. "I've read the notes on my treasures. I know there is nothing special about this. Alexander only wore it for a single day."

Master Abelard smiled a slow smile, one that I know well.

"You underestimate me, Gerald. It was I who provided this armband to your brother, and not simply because Cyril was desperate to come up with a gift for you for your seventh Hatchday. I wanted you to have this in your possession. *This* armband is no mere one-day wonder. Alexander wore it in many battles, and it is imbued with his strength and his spirit. I am going to put it around your upper foreleg. When I do, the strength of Alexander himself will join with yours! This will give you power and confidence to do what must be done. Are you ready for it?"

Humbled, awed, I nodded.

Master Abelard wrapped the bronze band around my right upper foreleg.

As Izzikiah is my witness, I felt strength and power descend upon me!

"Are you ready for the journey?" asked Master A.

"I am ready to fly to Mars if need be!" I replied.

"That's my good student! That's the griffling I have been teaching these last years!"

At that point I would have done anything for him.

ALERT
From: The High Council of New Batavia
To: All Households, Levels I, II, and III
Date: July 8

Householders—

As you undoubtedly know by this time, New Batavia is in danger of inundation. Though we are still hoping to avert the catastrophe that will occur should the humans proceed with their Wetlands Preservation Project, our chances are dimming.

The threat is not immediate, and we will have warning. However, we are asking that everyone begin preparing to leave the city at a moment's notice. Plan on bringing only your most treasured possessions and whatever money you have at hand.

As always, once Up Above, secrecy will be essential. For this reason please carefully review the pamphlet "Rules for Aboveground Behavior." We are aware that most of you have not felt a need to consult this booklet for many decades. But if the entire city is forced aboveground, these guidelines will be essential to avoiding discovery . . . which is essential to our survival!

Hieronymus Bronk
Mayor

7/8

Holy mouthwatering, fresh-baked snickerdoodles, was that an adventure!

Our hope was to accomplish this in a single night—for Gerald and me to travel to the Enchanted Realm, capture the rabbits, and return to New Batavia, all before dawn.

After the skylamps had dimmed for the evening, Karel Hummel led Gerald and me to the shrinking/enlarging stairway. Bibi and Herb wanted to come to see us off, but Karel insisted that the fewer beings involved, the better. I think he was probably right.

I knew Karel believed what we were doing was necessary and important. I also understood that he was putting himself in personal danger by opening that door, as we had not been cleared to return to the Up Above. If we didn't succeed, if something happened so that we didn't make it back, he would be in for severe punishment.

According to Bibi, who had been out walking around, the mood in New Batavia had become nasty and grim. Everyone was blaming everyone else for the approaching calamity, and only a few bold voices were calling for wise preparation against the looming disaster.

The trip back up the magic stairway was as disturbing, in a reverse kind of way, as the trip down had been. I constantly felt that . . . well, that the whole world was sucking at me, pulling me apart.

But I wasn't coming apart, just getting bigger.

When Gerald and I stepped out of the tree, we were our normal size.

"What now?" Gerald asked.

"Back to the farmhouse to get Bibi's gloves. Then we walk to the church and go to the Enchanted Realm!"

I was quivering with excitement . . . and almost paralyzed with fear.

Wednesday, July 8

I didn't write anything yesterday because I was too exhausted. But now I can tell my part of the story . . . which I am itching to do.

When we got back to Brad's home, it was clear I couldn't fit through the door of the farmhouse. So I had to wait in the barn while Brad fetched the gloves.

I was in a state of high fuss—excited to be returning to the Realm but also terrified of what would happen when we got there. Would I be discovered? Caught? Imprisoned for fleeing to the human world? (Not to mention having been seen!)

And Izzikiah alone knows what the consequences might be for bringing a human in with me!

The truth was, we couldn't let such a discovery happen. If I was detained, the entire city of New Batavia was going to end up underwater! Oh, the gnomes would almost certainly get out before that happened. But they would lose their homes and almost everything they owned.

More than that, they would lose the underground world they had worked for centuries to create! An entire city, drowned.

And once that happened, it was almost certain they would be discovered. It's one thing to hide from the human world by only coming out at night, and only in small numbers. It would be an entirely different thing to suddenly have over *six thousand* gnomes living aboveground! Someone would certainly find them. And what would come of that?

I was so lost in my thoughts I didn't hear Brad approach until he said, "Gerald?"

I leaped into the air with a squawk and was immediately embarrassed for having done so. That was the old me, not the one who wore Alexander's armband!

Brad was kind enough not to laugh. All he said was "Ready?"

"Ready, steady, and ready," I answered, using Master Abelard's phrase.

So we set off. It was after midnight, and there was unlikely to be any traffic on the little country road. Even so, we stayed well to the side of the road, walking through the woods. It would not do to be spotted, not for either of us.

It took about half an hour to reach the little church where we would make our transit back to the Enchanted Realm.

"I have to say, going through the Transcendental Curtain this way is going to be easier than the method I used to enter the human world!" I told Brad.

He looked at me oddly but said nothing.

We stood in front of the church door, then turned

right and began to walk. Master Abelard and Bibi had stressed that we must keep the church to our left as we went around it.

One circuit of the church and nothing happened. But then nothing was supposed to happen at that point. I was just fussing.

As we finished the second circuit I heard Brad mutter, "I hope this works."

So I was not the only one who was fussing.

I did begin to worry as we made the third circuit. I was expecting some kind of feeling . . . though I didn't know what kind of feeling it would be.

Then . . . ZING! It wasn't in the least gradual, as I had thought it would be. Instead, when we reached the front of the church and passed exactly over the spot where we had started, the transition happened. One second we were in the human world. Before we finished the next step, we were in the Enchanted Realm!

"Yow!" cried Brad. "That tingles! Do you recognize this place, Gerald?"

I didn't answer.

I was too shocked by who was waiting for us.

7/8 (continued)

I can honestly say I have never seen a greater look of shock than when Gerald and I entered the Enchanted Realm and he found his sister waiting for him.

"Violet!" cried Gerald while I was still trying to deal with the tingling, which was like the pins and needles your foot gets when it goes to sleep, except I had it from head to toe. "What are you doing here?"

"Waiting for you," his sister said sharply. "It's about time you came back. Mom and Dad are having fits."

"But how could you possibly know I would come through at this very spot?"

"I didn't know for certain. But Dad went to the university and threatened to eat someone if they didn't give him some information about where you might have gone. They finally sent him to your teacher's best friend, some guy named Henrik. He told Dad the spots most likely for you to reappear if you *did* decide to return. We've been keeping watch on those places ever since."

"Are you going to have me arrested?" Gerald asked.

His sister looked at him as if he were crazy. "Gerald, you are my brother . . . my triplet! Do you really think I'd do that? Besides, Mom and Dad would never forgive me. Now, tell me what you've gotten yourself into. And why you have a human with you! What's its name?"

"He's not an it," replied Gerald indignantly. "He's a

boy, and his name is Bradley . . . though if you're nice, he'll let you call him Brad."

Violet turned to look me over. "I never saw a human before," she said. "You don't look as strange as I expected. Thank you for helping my brother."

"You're welcome," I said, not entirely comfortable in her gaze.

"Now, tell me what you're up to," said Violet.

Stammering and stuttering, Gerald explained our plan to gather a batch of pink bunnies to take to the human world so we could save New Batavia from drowning.

"I love that idea!" she cried when he was finished.

Gerald looked at her as if she had just said, "Please hit me on the head with a brick a dozen times."

"You do?"

"Yes! It's completely worthy and might even help us secure a tenth treasure."

"Us? I thought you had your tenth treasure all figured out," said Gerald. I noticed that he sounded a bit . . . well, bitter.

Lowering her head, Violet said, "I did, but it fell through."

"How come you never talked to me about it?" he asked.

"Because we were supposed to do it on our own, you big doot! But time is getting tight, so I think we should all work together."

"All?" said Gerald, clearly puzzled.

"You and me and Cyril."

"Cyril doesn't have his tenth treasure, either?" yelped Gerald.

Violet shook her head, then said, "Look, I know Cyril can be kind of a pain. But he is our brother. Maybe he could help."

Gerald tilted his head in that way I was getting to know and said, "Won't you both get into big trouble for this?"

"Hard to say, but maybe not. Mom and Dad and Cyril and I have spent a lot of time talking to that Henrik guy. It turns out some of the rules of the Enchanted Realm are more confusing and more subtle—that was his word for it, 'subtle'—than we thought. The most important thing right now is to get our tenth treasures."

She closed her eyes and shivered. "Gerald, if we don't manage that, our Tenth Hatchday Ceremony is going to be a disaster. Which will kind of kill Dad. Cyril and I have been frantic about it."

She paused, and I could tell the next words were hard for her. "I know Cyril and I were kind of rough on you, and I'm sorry. I was a brat sister. Of course, you were a stinky brother, but that's not enough of an excuse. I will tell you the truth: Cyril and I are both amazed you had the griffin guts to leave the Enchanted Realm. All of a sudden you feel like the big brother we always wanted."

Gerald spread his wings to their full width (which was stunning), then bowed. He pressed his beak to his sister's talons and murmured, "My dearest Violet, I am sorry to have brought shame to our family by being first laid but

★

last hatched. However, now I have a mission, and a worthy one. I would be honored to have you and Cyril join me."

Then he straightened his shoulders, raised his head, and cried, "Overflights unite!"

"Overflights unite!" Violet repeated. Then she said, "It's really good you came through at the spot where I've been watching. If you had come through where either Mom or Dad is waiting, you would have had no chance of returning to the human world, gnome emergency or not. Mom has been frantic. Dad has been, well . . ."

"Well WHAT?" Gerald demanded.

"It's like he doesn't know what to think. He's very worried. And he's upset because Mom's upset, which of course makes life miserable for everyone. But I also get the feeling he's proud of you for doing something so daring. Only, he can't admit that in front of Mom. I'm going to go get Cyril. Do you promise to stay here? No, forget that. Come with me. It will be faster."

"But I can't leave Brad here," Gerald said.

"Well, let him ride on your back."

"I can't do that!"

Violet sighed in exasperation. "Then how were you planning to get him back to the human world?"

"Oh," said Gerald in a small voice. "I guess I hadn't thought about that." He turned toward me. "Are you all right with this, Brad?"

I told him I'd been planning on it all along.

"How did you know?" he asked, sounding startled.

"Your teacher told me."

"Why didn't he mention it to me?"

Violet rolled her eyes. "He probably didn't think he needed to! Honestly, Gerald, for the smart one in the family you don't always think things through. Come on. Let's go get Cyril and catch some bunnies!"

Gerald crouched and said, "Climb on!"

I positioned myself in front of his wings. "What should I hold on to?" I asked, wishing I had a saddle.

"Lean forward and grab my neck. But don't squeeze!"

I did as he instructed.

"Let's *go*!" urged Violet.

Gerald climbed to the top of a nearby boulder, leaped into the air, and began to beat his mighty wings.

In an instant we were flying! I felt a surge of joy and whooped with delight. This was the most awesome thing ever!

The bright light of the massive, nearly full moon revealed the wild and craggy world below me.

The air around us was pure and cool.

The rhythmic beat of Gerald's wings was a beautiful sound.

I wanted to fly forever!

With Bradley mounted on my neck, flying was considerably more difficult than usual. Fortunately, it only took about ten minutes to reach the place where Cyril was stationed.

I had expected to be nervous about seeing my brother and was surprised that I wasn't. Then I realized that of course I wouldn't be nervous, since I was wearing Alexander's armband.

I wondered, then, if Cyril had any idea what an amazing treasure he had actually given me. And why did Master Abelard never tell me about it before? I suppose he was waiting until I really needed it. Maybe it would have been a mistake to wear it while trying to fly through the cliff that took us to the human world . . . it might have made me so brave that I wouldn't have felt a need to believe, in which case I might have crashed and died!

Master A is wise indeed.

To my satisfaction, it was Cyril who let out a squawk when Violet and I landed in front of him. "Gerald, where have you been?" he cried. "And what in the name of Izzikiah are you doing with a human on your back?" He squinted, then said, "That is a human, right?"

"Yes, he's a human. His name is Bradley, and he has come to help us with an important task."

Then Violet and I explained the plans for the Great Bunny Hunt and asked if he wanted to help.

"Count me in!" Cyril cried. "I love catching bunnies!"

"You have to promise not to eat them," Violet said.

"Not even one?" Cyril asked mournfully.

"Not even one," I said. "Or aren't you strong enough of will to resist? If that's the case, we can't use you."

"I can do it!" said Cyril.

"Overflights unite!" cried Violet.

"Overflights unite!" Cyril and I shouted together.

And so it was that the Great Bunny Hunt began.

The Overflight Bunny Hunt

Though Clan Overflight is a solid member of the Northern Quarter of the North American Aerie, historically it has been a quiet family, with little to distinguish it.

This ended, however, when with daring and élan the current younger generation carried out a bold plan to help an endangered city of gnomes who had been living in self-imposed exile in the human world. (That is as much on the matter as I am allowed to record here.)

In brief, Gerald, Violet, and Cyril Overflight captured twenty-four of the famous Cherry Blossom Hares of the Northern Quarter. They were aided in this by a human boy, Bradley Ashango.

Bradley had befriended Gerald, the oldest of the Overflight triplets (or perhaps the youngest . . . there is some confusion on this matter), who had brought the boy with him *into* the Enchanted Realm! A daring move, indeed!

Catching the rabbits was fairly easy for the three grifflings, as they were skilled hunters. The greater task lay in the self-control it took for them to *not* devour their prey in the moment of capture. Rather than disemboweling and consuming their catches, the grifflings brought them to the Ashango boy, who took each rabbit and stored it in a gnome-woven mesh bag.

To the human's credit he was very careful with the creatures, putting no more than four in each bag.

When the hunt ended, the Overflights had captured two dozen rabbits.

However, if the hunt was easy, the journey to the human world was fraught with unexpected peril.

Adelaide Hornbeam, Dwarf
Record Keeper, North American Aerie

7/8 (continued)

While Gerald and his siblings hunted, I was assigned to wait at the place where we had met Cyril. The griffling triplets were to bring their catches to me for safekeeping.

I felt a surge of pride when Gerald was the first to return. In his talons he clutched, as promised, a pink bunny.

Holy rabbit stew, it was the biggest freaking bun-creature I had ever seen!

Not so big that people wouldn't believe it was real. Just . . . *huge.*

And it was definitely pink. Not cotton-candy pink, not valentine pink. Just . . . pink. As in, its fur had a mild but definite tint, kind of like the light pink rosebuds in Bibi's flower garden.

It wasn't until I saw that first bunny that I really believed my plan might work. No one in the human world could doubt that this rabbit was a species that had never been seen before!

Soon Violet and Cyril returned with pink rabbits as well. I carefully took each rabbit from their talons, while the raptor-captor repeated over and over, "I must not eat this bunny. I must not eat this bunny!"

Then I would place the wriggling critter into one of the bags Gerald and I had brought from New Batavia.

I could fit four bunnies into a bag without overcrowding. Since each of the griffins could carry two bags, we topped out at twenty-four bunnies (eight bunnies times three griffins).

It was time to head back to the human world.

Which was when our real troubles began.

As I had flown through the solid cliff face once, I was much less worried about doing it this time. Cyril and Violet, however, almost backed out at that point.

"Do you mean to tell me you're afraid?" I asked, trying not to show how thoroughly I enjoyed the question.

"Certainly not!" said Cyril. "It's more that, um . . . I'm worried about what Mom and Dad will think when they can't find us!"

"We can leave a note, like I did the first time," I said.

"But we don't have any paper," protested Violet.

"I can take a page out of my pocket journal," Brad replied.

The sibs didn't look pleased, but in the end that was what we did. We placed the note exactly where Cyril had been stationed, holding it down with a rock so it wouldn't blow away. Mom and Dad were sure to find it when they came looking for him.

That done, we started toward the Cliff of Passage.

"Do you know the way?" Brad asked. He sounded a bit nervous.

"Of course," I said, speaking more confidently than I felt. That was probably an effect of Alexander's armband. In truth, I was not entirely certain I could spot the right cliff, since I had been in such a state of high fuss when Master Abelard and I first approached it.

I wondered how I could be positive. I couldn't fly into the wrong cliff! I wouldn't just be killing myself. Brad would perish as well. And New Batavia would be drowned.

As I flew in what I *thought* was the right direction, Brad was spotting landmarks and assuring me that I was indeed on track. There were two places where I was not quite sure, but Brad said, "Yes, that jagged peak should be to our right," then "No, Gerald, turn right here . . . yes, head toward the rock face with the red streak in it."

And then there was no more need for directions, no more need for doubt.

We knew we had come to the right place, because it was guarded.

By a dragon.

7/8 (continued)

Holy smoldering hot sauce! When I saw that dragon flying back and forth in front of the Cliff of Passage, I thought I was going to wet my pants. In an instant this trip to the Enchanted Realm had turned from dream journey to blazing nightmare!

And I do mean blazing, since the monster shot fire from its mouth, then bellowed, "Who seeks to use this passage to the human world must first deal with me, Zarnakk!"

Zarnakk had to be forty feet long. In the moonlight I could see that the creature's scales were bronzy scarlet. Its batlike wings were three times as long as Gerald. Its enormous eyes, emerald green, seemed to burn with an inner fire.

To my astonishment, Gerald let out a loud "Gaaah!" then shouted, "Why do you wish to stop us, Zarnakk?"

"For the sake of a toll. I know from the gossip in these parts that this passageway was used recently. And I know from experience that once used, the cliff is often used again shortly after. But I have no reason to allow free passage in my territory. And make no mistake, this cliff is in *my* territory. So what do you have to offer me?"

"We cannot negotiate while flying," Gerald replied.

I was amazed at how calm my friend sounded.

"Then meet me on that triangular peak below and to your right," Zarnakk answered. "Do not think to fool me or fly past me. My flames are long, and I will roast you until the savory smell of your burning flesh brings hungry ghouls out to feast on you."

And I thought the bullies at school were bad! That was the nastiest thing I had ever heard anyone say!

"I think it is safe for us to land," said Gerald, speaking so only I could hear. "Dragons are fierce, but they are bonded to negotiate in good faith."

We touched down on the peak, Cyril and Violet not far behind us. Once we were there, Zarnakk settled on the opposite side. The beast's head was large enough that I was pretty sure it could swallow me in a single bite. I couldn't tell if it was male or female, and didn't know which would be more frightening. Either way, my terrified heart was threatening to pound its way out of my chest.

Gerald, on the other hand, was remarkably calm, which probably kept me from totally freaking out.

In a voice that sounded like it came from inside an enormous copper kettle, Zarnakk said, "Why do you wish to pass to the human world? And what in the name of the Great Dragon are you doing with those rabbits?"

"We are on a rescue mission," Gerald said, his voice firm, bold, and courageous.

The dragon snorted, which resulted in a short burst of flame. "Rescuing what?"

"We seek to save a city of gnomes from discovery by humans," Gerald replied. Then he gave a brief description of the situation.

"Sounds like nonsense to me," Zarnakk snarled. "However, I am willing to let you pass . . . if you have something to pay the toll."

"What is the toll?" asked Gerald.

The dragon shrugged its massive wings. "Something of value. Something you have that I want. The human would be a good possibility. I haven't had human for supper in a long time."

I nearly fainted at those words. And I was enormously relieved when Gerald answered, "That is not possible. Name something else."

"What do you have? And don't tell me rabbits! I am not interested in snack food. I want something of value!"

After a long silence, Gerald surprised me by saying, "I can give you my armband. It was worn by Alexander the Great."

"No!" Violet cried. "You can't give up one of your treasures!"

"I'll do what I have to do," Gerald answered, his voice grim.

Zarnakk laughed again. "I know about those armbands, griffin. Alexander wore one every day for years. They're common as mice."

"Not this one," Gerald replied. "This is a rare and special armband. Alexander wore it during many battles, and it is imbued with his spirit."

"A likely story," snorted the dragon.

"Actually, I think it's true," said Violet. "Gerald is my brother and he's always been kind of a siss . . ." She paused, and I could tell she was looking for a word that wouldn't be too insulting. "He's always been very . . . shy. I am astonished at the way he has been speaking to you."

"Me too," Cyril put in. "I think that armband *must* have special powers. I've never heard Gerald talk like this."

I heard a note of admiration in Cyril's voice and hoped that Gerald caught it, too.

"Very well," said Zarnakk. "I accept the armband in return for passage through the cliff."

"Bradley?" whispered Gerald.

I knew what he was asking. I slid from his back, then removed the bronze band from his foreleg. I heard him choke back a sigh as I did.

I carried the armband to the dragon. It was, hands down, the single most terrifying thing I ever have done. As I got closer the heat was almost more than I could bear. Green, yellow, and red flames flickered around the edges of the creature's nostrils, which were so big I could have stuck my head inside them.

When I was close enough, the dragon stretched its

massive claws forward. With surprising delicacy, it took the bronze band from my trembling fingers.

I backed away quickly.

"You may pass!" roared the dragon.

Then it spread its enormous wings and flew away.

WANTED

Zarnakk the dragon, for unauthorized blockade of Passage Point through the Transcendental Curtain; unauthorized collection of toll.

Reward is offered for information regarding his whereabouts.

Wednesday, July 8 (continued)

I had felt completely calm while negotiating with the dragon, but as soon as Brad removed the armband I nearly collapsed in terror.

I was not sure I could make it through the cliff now, even though I had done it once already. It felt as if all my courage had gone with the armband. Making it worse was the grief and guilt that I felt for having given up one of my treasures!

Before I could tell the others I wasn't sure I could go on, Cyril said, "That was amazing, Gerald. How did you think up such a good lie so quickly?"

"What lie?" I asked, puzzled.

"About the armband, of course!"

"That wasn't a lie," I said. "Master Abelard told me the armband's true power just before we came here."

Cyril laughed. "I always thought that gnome was kind of shifty. Listen, Gerald, I tried the armband on before I gave it to you. There was nothing magic about it."

I was staggered by this. Not because Master A had lied to me. I had already learned that he was deceitful. What startled me was what Violet now put into words: "Gerald, that means that all the boldness you've been showing came from you."

I shook my wings and stood up straight.

"Overflights unite!" I cried. "Through the cliff!"

Brad climbed back onto my neck. Then I launched myself into the air. Using all my strength, I hurtled forward at top speed, struck the stone wall, and went straight through.

I heard Brad scream, but I guess his belief was not required.

Moments later Violet and Cyril popped through after me.

"We did it!" cried Violet.

"Follow me!" I ordered. (Which I now realize was kind of silly—what else were they going to do?)

We had not been flying for more than five minutes when a ray of green light flashed past.

"Lasers!" shouted Brad. "Dive! *Dive!*"

"Cyril! Violet! Get as close to the treetops as you can!" I ordered as I headed downward.

More flashes of green light—and a shriek of pain from Cyril! "My butt!" he shrieked. "Something got me in the butt!"

"Dive!" repeated Brad.

Soon we were skimming above the treetops, below the sight of this terrible "radar" and the things that fired "lasers."

I led the way back to the field behind Brad's house, where we touched down.

"My butt really hurts!" complained Cyril.

"You've been wounded in the line of duty," Violet said. "You can take pride in that!" Then she looked around and said, "Great Izzikiah, we're actually in the human world."

"Hope we don't get into too much trouble for this," muttered Cyril.

We made our way back to the tree that led to New Batavia, where we found Karel Hummel waiting for us.

"I was too nervous to stay below," he explained as he opened the doorway that led us back to the underground city.

I warned my siblings about the pressure they would feel, and then we started down to New Batavia, bunnies and all.

NEW BATAVIA
TOWN CRIER

JULY 9

CRISIS AVERTED?

By Marta Joosten

    The city received unexpected good news today on the matter of the wetlands project that has threatened to destroy our homes. In a daring move, two of our guests—Gerald Overflight and Bradley Ashango—made an unauthorized exit to Up Above and then journeyed to the Enchanted Realm.

    There, with the help of Gerald's siblings, Violet and Cyril, they caught some two dozen pink rabbits that our friends from the Gnome Protective Association are confident can be used to convince the authorities that the wetlands project must go to its second-choice location.

    While everyone in New Batavia is enormously relieved by this development, what the youngsters have done is not free of controversy.

    First off, there is the matter of their leaving New Batavia without permission. "They were here under protective guard until it was determined whether it was safe to allow them to return to the human world. They had no business leaving, no matter how supposedly noble were their intentions," thundered Councilman Pieter de Muis, who is demanding a complete investigation of the covert operation.

Compounding the situation is the fact that the youngsters took with them a brass armband once worn by Alexander the Great, which was one of the "treasures" that had been deposited as bond for the griffin's tutor, Abelard Chronicus, who is still awaiting trial for his unauthorized entry into New Batavia.

There is a further complication. It appears, though it is not confirmed, that Overflight and Ashango were aided in leaving the city by Karel Hummel, the very gnome who had been in charge of bringing them in.

There is a suspicion that it was also Hummel who obtained the armband for them.

The armband has not been returned. According to the griffins, it was used in the Enchanted Realm to pay a toll to a dragon.

The city council will be meeting tonight to determine how to deal with these issues. The meeting is open to all citizens.

7/9

By the god of fresh-baked apple pies, I swear my Bibi is the best! Not only did she mail the journal entries for me, she actually wrote a couple of new ones to keep me up-to-date!

"It wasn't hard to copy the style," she said drily. Then she gave me a look and added, "Can you tell me why you are pretending to be a simpleton?"

I decided to put it on the line. "I got tired of getting beat up for being smart. I had enough of that at the last school. I didn't want it to continue this year."

Bibi took that in for a second, then said, "I think your mother and I need to have a little talk with your school before the fall session begins. And with you, too." But that was all she said about it, since we had much bigger issues to deal with—namely, the meeting of the city council that night. Gerald and I broke a lot of rules for the Pink Bunny Adventure, and it turns out that not everyone is happy about it.

Honest to Pete, I get the impression that some of these gnomes think following the rules is more important than saving their city from drowning!

In other news: The gnomes are taking care of Cyril's wounded backside. He was lucky in that the laser only grazed his butt. But it did burn off a line of fur. The gnomes say it might not grow back.

★   ★

I get the feeling he is secretly proud of having a scar earned during an adventure.

The triplets seem to be getting along quite well. I can tell that Gerald is pleased but cautious. He is probably afraid of more teasing. But it's clear that Violet and Cyril are now looking at him as their leader.

July 9

The meeting was called to order at eight p.m. by Mayor Bronk.

The regularly scheduled agenda was set aside for a discussion of the Incident of the Pink Rabbits.

The conversation was . . . lively. Some felt that there should be swift punishment for those who left the colony without permission and for anyone who was involved in helping them, most specifically Karel Hummel. Councilman de Muis, in particular, was adamant that while this event may have had a good result, the failure to go through proper channels was an insult to the colony and its leadership, and those involved should be punished.

However, the great majority of speakers were in favor of the endeavor. In the end, a vote was made to present the three griffins and the human boy with medals of honor for their efforts in saving the city from a watery doom. And, having been proved true friends of New Batavia, they are now free to come and go as they wish. They will always be welcome in our midst.

Respectfully submitted,

Elsa Vanderhoff
City Scribe

Friday, July 10

I have earned my tenth treasure!

It is a medal . . . a gold medal!

This is a matter of great pride.

However, I have also lost one of my treasures, which is a matter of great shame.

I do not know if I can go back to the Enchanted Realm.

"You have to come back," Violet has been insisting. "Mom and Dad will go nuts if you don't."

Even Cyril wants me to come back!

Here is today's poem:

Every night, every day,
I feel terror and hope.
If I do head for home
Will I be able to cope?

I am so proud of what I have done.

I am so fearful of going home.

Notice of Banishment

On this day, July 10, let it be known that for his defiance of authority, his insistence on pursuing forbidden research, and his numerous lies and deceits—as revealed by the ongoing investigation into his life and work—the gnome Abelard Chronicus is henceforth to be spoken of as "Abelard Chronicus, Rogue."

That is, when he is spoken of at all.

This should be rare, as Abelard Chronicus, Rogue, is no longer welcome at the University Enchantica.

As a result, it is the decision of the High Council of the North American Realm that Abelard Chronicus, Rogue, shall be evermore banished to the place to which he has departed . . . a place that, as per the rules of the Council, shall not be named in this document!

Signed,

Bromphys Strunk, Troll
Chief Legal Officer
Enchanted Realm
North America

From the Notebook of Abelard Chronicus

◇◇◇◇◇◇◇◇◇◇◇◇◇◇◇◇◇◇◇◇◇

July 11

The order of banishment came today. It was not unexpected. Even so, I will admit that it stung a bit to read the thing.

On the other hand, it also gave me a chuckle, as I am ordered to remain in the very place that I've been seeking for nearly three centuries!

Eduard and I raised a tankard of the city's excellent gnome ale over that tonight.

It is so good to have my twin back! And I've been offered a job teaching at the school. It's not a university-level position, but I think I can be happy working with young people for the rest of my life.

Alas, I shall be losing Gerald as a student. He is returning to the Enchanted Realm tonight.

I shall miss the griffling. I take pride in the fact that he has grown and performed beyond all my expectations.

In the end, I think this trip was good for him.

Or is that merely self-justification?

(Summer Assignment)

7/14

I met a griffin in my grandmother's barn. He was big and fierce-looking. But he was also kind of a scaredy-cat.

We made friends. We went on an adventure together. It was frightening but fun.

Now the griffin has gone home. I miss him. A lot.

(3 paragraphs, 3 sentences each.)

7/14

I have not felt like writing here for a while.

That's because Gerald and his sibs left for the Enchanted Realm three nights ago.

I hadn't realized how much I would miss him.

The night of their departure, Bibi and I walked the triplets to the church. We didn't talk much while we were walking.

It's easy to be quiet in the dark, at night.

And, to be honest, I didn't know what to say.

When we reached the transit point, Bibi used my cell to take a picture of me with the three griffins.

Then it was time for them to go.

"You two go first," Gerald told Violet and Cyril. "I want to talk to Bradley for a little bit."

"Oh no!" Violet replied. "If we come home without you, Mom and Dad will skin us alive!"

"I'll come through in a few minutes," Gerald promised. "This passage point will bring you through to where Violet was waiting. But Mom and Dad should be waiting where Cyril was stationed, since that is where we left the note for them. Wait for me to come through, and we will fly to greet them together."

"I will make certain Gerald keeps his promise to join you," Bibi said.

That satisfied Violet and Cyril, since when Bibi makes a promise you just know she is going to keep it.

It was interesting to watch Cyril and Violet go widdershins around the church. To be more precise, it wasn't the *going* that was so fascinating. It was the moment when they completed the third circuit and then vanished right before our eyes! As they did I heard a snapping sound that reminded me of lightning. A sharp, pleasant odor lingered behind them.

Bibi looked at Gerald and me. "I'll give you two a few minutes to say good-bye," she said. Then she stepped back into the woods that grow up to the edge of the church lawn.

"Well," said Gerald.

"Well," I said.

"I'm going to miss you," he whispered.

"I'm going to miss you," I replied.

I was trying hard not to cry. But I so much didn't want him to go! I don't have many friends, and I had never had a friend like Gerald. He was funny and fussy and I would trust him with my life. Heck, I *had* trusted him with my life! Even though we hadn't known each other all that long, it was hard to think of life without him. How can you experience something like meeting a griffin and then just have it all be over, gone, ended?

When my father died, I had stopped believing that good things could ever happen to me.

Then Gerald happened and proved me wrong. He brought magic back into my life. He made me believe again . . . believe that I could be happy.

And now he was going away.

"Can I have a hug?" he whispered.

I didn't know it was possible to hug a griffin, but I was willing to try. I stepped forward and put my arms around his neck.

He wrapped his wings around me, then rested his beak on my shoulder and whispered, "Thank you, Bradley Ashango."

I hugged him tighter and replied, "Thank you, Gerald Overflight!"

We let each other go, and he went widdershins around the church three times.

After he was gone, Bibi and I walked home in silence.

She kept an arm around my shoulder all the way.

That night I cried myself to sleep.

THE NEW YORK TIMES

PINK RABBITS FOUND
IN UPSTATE TOWN

By Barbara Block

The small town of Vande Velde's Landing, mostly known for its claim to be host to a colony of gnomes, has a new bit of fanciful lore to add to its repertoire: pink rabbits!

The rabbits were first noticed by Agatha Riddlehoover, who spotted them in her garden. Using a live-catch trap, Mrs. Riddlehoover gathered three of the rabbits and brought them to a town meeting.

Not surprisingly, people assumed that the creatures were some sort of hoax, most likely white rabbits that had been dyed pink.

However, at Mrs. Riddlehoover's insistence, genetic testing was done.

To the astonishment of everyone,

except perhaps Mrs. Riddlehoover, the rabbits are indeed a unique species.

This discovery has serious potential to impact a wetlands preservation project that was scheduled for the area, one that would have affected the acreage next to Mrs. Riddlehoover's farm. She has been a longtime opponent of the plan, which was one reason there was so much skepticism about the rabbits when she brought them in.

Due to their unique gene sequence, the rabbits will almost certainly qualify as an endangered species. Once this is certified, the wetlands project will have to move to the second-choice location, which is far from Mrs. Riddlehoover's farm.

She claims, for reasons that are unclear, that this will be the best solution for everyone.

Tuesday, July 14

I have been neglecting my diary because I am in such a state of fuss.

So now I need to do some catching up.

To begin with, the sibs and I returned to the Enchanted Realm three nights ago.

As expected, we came through at the exact place Violet had been waiting for me on my first return.

I had asked C and V to go ahead of me so I could say good-bye to Bradley in private.

I wanted to be alone for that. I knew, even before attempting it, that it would be hard to let go of a friend now that I had finally made one.

It was a moment my heart will never forget.

Once I had rejoined the sibs, we flew to Cyril's watch spot.

Also as expected, our parents were there, waiting for us.

Many things were said then, an odd mix of "How could you?" and "Thank goodness you're safe!" and "Do you have any idea how worried we were?" and "We're so relieved!"

Mom was madder than Dad, but she also cried more.

Dad seemed oddly proud . . . especially when we showed him our medals.

"We all have our tenth treasure!" said Violet excitedly.

"And we earned them, really earned them!" added Cyril.

"But Gerald was the leader," said Violet. "That's why his is gold and ours are silver. Also, Cyril has a special ribbon on his, because he was wounded in action!"

Dad was jubilant until I said, "I have still shamed us, Father. I lost one of my treasures, on the homeward trip after the hunt. So I still have only nine."

"Lost a treasure?!" squawked Dad, as if it was the most horrifying thing he had ever heard.

Which it probably was.

Tomorrow is our Hatchday. Well, it is Violet and Cyril's Hatchday. Mine does not come until the day after, though to avoid embarrassment to the family, we have always celebrated as if we hatched on the same day.

It is a day I am now dreading.

Especially considering the invitations that have gone out . . .

You Are Invited!

It is with enormous pride that Reginald and Cecelia Overflight invite you to the Tenth Hatchday celebration of their beloved triplets, Gerald, Violet, and Cyril.

Place: Great Cavern of the Griffin Stronghold of the Northern Quarter

Time: Festivities begin when the sun is directly overhead. (Note: Overnight accommodations are available for trolls and other sun-sensitive beings.)

Schedule: First two hours will be for display of the grifflings' hoards, including their Tenth Hatchday treasures, as required of each of the triplets.

Next we will be treated to remarks by Artoremus Lashtail, High Lord of the Griffin Stronghold of the Northern Quarter.

Following Lord Lashtail's remarks will be a reception, with refreshments provided by the Lower Moldavian Dwarfs.

Note: Cavern lighting provided as a special gift to the family by the Granite Valley Trolls.

Wednesday, July 15

This morning Violet and Cyril and I rose and groomed ourselves. Then we flew as a family to the Great Cavern of the Northern Aerie, which is where everyone's Tenth Hatchday Ceremony takes place.

All of our friends and relatives were there, as is customary. The Granite Valley Trolls had sent a small group to light the cavern, in honor of their long and happy connection to our clan.

At the rear of the cave, on a long shelf of stone, our treasures had been laid out for all to admire. Though none would dare think to steal one, three of our cousins stood guard, because that is what griffins do. We are guardians of treasure.

Presiding over the day was the High Lord of the Griffin Stronghold of the Northern Quarter, Artoremus Lashtail himself.

I wanted to die.

But something odd was happening.

My cousins were congratulating me!

Why would they be congratulating me when I had failed so spectacularly?

I discovered the answer when the sibs and I went to stand behind our treasures, in order that we might explain them to the community. My brass armband was there!

Not only that, there was something else that I had never before seen at a Tenth Hatchday gathering.

I had been granted my Certificate of Independence!

I am no longer a griffling! And I have skipped right over being a griffer. I am officially a griffin, free to come and go from our aerie as I wish!

I was so startled, I could hardly focus on Artoremus Lashtail's speech.

Well, to be honest, his speeches are so long hardly anyone can focus on them. But I kept wondering what had happened, how this had come to be!

All was explained at the party afterward when I rushed to my parents.

Mom's eyes twinkling, she said, "Gerald Overflight, if you ever again scare me like you did this last week, I will do more than keep good news from you! You had that little fright coming, my son."

"But what happened?"

My father chuckled. "Zarnakk was spotted demanding a toll for passage by one of the other dragons. This is actually forbidden by the dragon code, and he had to surrender your armband. It was brought back to us two days ago."

"And the Certificate of Independence?" I asked.

"That was decreed by Artoremus Lashtail when he heard the entire story of your adventures," said my mother.

So there it is. Instead of ten treasures, as I needed, and nine, as I feared, I now possess *eleven* treasures!

Given how this all turned out, it is going to be hard for me to stay mad at Master Abelard.

Cyril and Violet are wildly jealous, of course.

I'm trying to control myself and not tease them about it too much.

7/18

I have started working on a novel about a boy who meets a griffin. Last night I was up late, editing the first chapter, when I heard a knocking at my window.

I looked up, then cried out in joy.

It was Gerald!

I flung open the window and stuck my head out.

"Meet me at the barn!" Gerald said.

"I'll be right there!"

"Good!" He banked left and glided toward the barn doors.

I threw on my clothes—I had been wearing my pajamas—and tiptoed down the stairs. (Bibi and Herb had gone to bed an hour earlier and I didn't want to wake them.)

Once I was out of the house, I pelted toward the barn.

"You came back!" I shouted, flinging my arms around Gerald. "You came back!"

"Yes," Gerald said proudly. "I have earned my Certificate of Independence and am now a griffin, not a griffling or a griffer. So I have a lot more freedom to do what I want. And what I wanted to do was come visit you."

"How long can you stay?" I asked.

"All summer! And not just this summer. I hope to come back every summer . . . at least, as long as you want me to. We can spend the summers together, Brad. I can live in the barn, if it's all right, but I should probably spend a lot of time in New Batavia so that I'm not detected here in the human world. But since you and I are now honorary citizens, we can go up or down the Enchanted Stair anytime we want."

"That's wonderful!" I cried, so excited and happy that I nearly started dancing.

"I hoped you'd think so," Gerald answered.

Then he crouched, grinned, and said, "Want to go for a ride?"

How could I resist?

I climbed on his back . . . and we took to the sky.

ABOUT THE AUTHOR

BRUCE COVILLE is the author of over one hundred books for children and young adults, including the international bestseller *My Teacher Is an Alien* and the wildly popular Unicorn Chronicles series. His work has appeared in more than a dozen languages and won children's choice awards in over a dozen states. He has been, at various times, a teacher, a toy maker, a magazine editor, a grave-digger, and a cookware salesman. He is also the founder of Full Cast Audio, an audiobook publishing company devoted to producing full cast, unabridged recordings of material for family listening. Mr. Coville lives in Syracuse, New York, with his wife, author and illustrator Katherine Coville. Visit him at BruceCoville.com and TheEnchantedFiles.com.

ABOUT THE ILLUSTRATOR

PAUL KIDBY is a self-taught artist whose first job was making false teeth. He eventually left the tooth business and became an illustrator. His work has appeared on computer game packaging, magazine covers, and bestselling books. Paul also enjoys sculpting, and his limited-edition bronzes are collected worldwide. Paul lives and works at his home studio in the south of England with his wife, Vanessa, and dog. When he is not painting, drawing, or sculpting, he is mostly found growing vegetables in his garden or walking in the countryside. Visit Paul at paulkidby.com.

LOOK FOR

The Enchanted Files

TROLLED

IN 2017!